Katherine's
LAST HOPE

DANIELLE M HAAS

To everyone who has ever had to start over. Keep living, keep hoping, keep loving.

1

___

Fatigue wove into the very fabric of Katherine Milton's being. She needed to get home to relieve her father of sitter duty, but her aching feet needed a few minutes of rest before heading to the parking lot. She dipped into the employee's lounge at the emergency room, taking a deep breath as she sank onto the soft cushions.

She tilted her head on the back of the couch and stared up at the ceiling. Exhaustion tempted her to close her eyes, but she feared she wouldn't open them before the sunrise.

Not like she'd sleep great anyway. Since Theo's accident the year before, she was lucky to get a solid two hours before being startled awake. That was always the worst part. Those brief seconds between waking from a dream and realizing the nightmare of her life—reaching for the familiar strength of her husband only to find the bed empty and cold.

Theo forever gone from this world.

A familiar pain twisted her insides like a knife, and she dashed away tears that never stopped.

"Long day?"

Dr. Jenna Spradling's concerned voice opened her eyes. If it were anyone else, she'd offer some kind of smile, but Jenna was more than a coworker. She was a friend who understood Katherine's daily struggles.

"Always." Sighing, she stood and stretched her hands above her head. "I need to get back to the house. Dad's there with Ollie. They're both probably fast asleep, but I still feel guilty keeping Dad there longer than necessary."

Since Theo's death, her father had been a Godsend. Hell, her entire community stood beside her daily, offering whatever support they could. But it was her father who'd given up his role as sheriff to step up and do whatever he could to help her navigate the shitty twist life had thrown her.

Jenna poured two cups of coffee then carried one to Katherine. "Did you put in overtime tonight? It's pretty late for you to still be here."

"Yeah." Katherine accepted the cup and took a small sip of the hot, bitter liquid. "What about you? You don't usually work the night shift."

"Someone called off," Jenna said with a small shrug. The movement caused the dark hair she'd pulled back in a low ponytail to sway. "I had most of the day at home, so I didn't mind picking up a shift. I spent a few hours at the shelter helping Mrs. Collins and Laura with a few new guests, then planted some flowers with Oliver. He loves getting his little hands dirty."

Katherine couldn't help but smile at the image of the messy little boy. Her own son was a few years older than Jenna's, and not only were their personalities similar, so were their names. Luckily, she called her Oliver Ollie most the time, erasing confusion when the two were together.

Which happened frequently as Katherine volunteered more time at the local women's shelter with Jenna. Something she'd hoped would stop her from focusing on her own problems. It didn't always work—nothing could keep her mind from wandering to Theo and the beautiful life they'd created—but it did strengthen the bond she had with so many amazing women in her community.

A village that came together for her time and time again.

"I promised my Ollie we could go to the nursery tomorrow. He always loves looking through the rows of plants and picking out something to grow." She frowned. "How were the new guests?"

Jenna shrugged. "Most of their wounds are on the inside, but I fixed the ones I could on the outside. Laura might need a hand tomorrow. I'll try and swing by, but I'm working a double shift."

"I'll call her," Katherine said. "I have the next two days off. Ollie can pick out some nice flowers for Mrs. Collins while we're out, then stop by the shelter. Do whatever needs doing."

A buzz sounded, and Jenna slipped her phone from her pocket. "Gotta go. I'll see you later."

"Thanks for the coffee," Katherine said, hoisting her cup in the air as Jenna retreated out the door.

She waited for her friend to leave before pouring the rest of her untouched drink down the drain. Most of the staff at the county hospital lived on caffeine, a habit she'd adopted right after graduating nursing school. But if she wanted even a prayer of getting any rest tonight, she couldn't drink any more. If she did, her nerves would be like live wires holding her hostage until the early morning light shone through her window.

With the cup disposed and sink rinsed, she snagged her jacket from where she'd hung it on the back of the hard chair. The mild spring weather promised warmer temperatures ahead, but the evening air still held a bite. She shrugged into the cream-colored fleece, secured her purse across her body, and made a beeline for the exit.

The emergency room waiting area was quiet, only the hum

of vending machines and drone of a small television kept the nurse at the front desk company. Katherine waved her goodbye to the young woman then waited for the automatic doors to whoosh open before stepping outside.

She inhaled a deep breath of crisp mountain air before strolling toward her car at the back of the mostly empty parking lot. Stars twinkled overhead and the outline of the Smoky Mountains in the distance looked more like a shadow drawn above the horizon than the jagged peaks she loved to hike.

She could take Ollie hiking over the next couple days. He used to love finding waterfalls off the well-traveled paths. Especially ones that poured into shallow streams he could splash around in. If the sun was out, it might be warm enough for such an adventure.

If she could convince him to go.

At seven, her son should be a ball of energy zipping through life and finding mischief. But the past year had taken a toll on the sad little boy. She struggled to wade through her own grief while keeping her precious son afloat, reminding him that it was okay to still have fun and enjoy their time together. Ollie placated her, but happiness and joy didn't reach his eyes the way it used to.

Maybe if she allowed him to bring a friend it would help coax him from his shell.

With a plan in place, she hurried across the lot. She reached into her purse for her keys, when something shifted in the air, raising the hair at the back of her neck.

Picking up the pace, she closed in on her vehicle. Why had she parked so far away knowing she'd be walking alone in the dark? The glow of a lamppost beamed down on her black SUV, but it didn't chase away the anxiety inching up her spine.

Five long strides. That's all it'd take to reach the handle and get inside, locking away whatever imaginary monsters chased her.

Four more steps.

Three.

She beeped her key fob to unlock the door. Her headlights flashed and she extended her arm for the handle.

A hard yank on her coat pulled her backward. An arm hooked around her neck and anchored her against a warm body. Something sharp and pointy found its way under the hem of her jacket and touched the tender spot just above her hipbone.

Hot moist breath skimmed her cheek, igniting her gag reflex.

"Don't do anything stupid, and I just might let you live."

COOL AIR FILTERED into Cody Hogan's cruiser as he drove down the country road toward the county hospital. Working as a sheriff's deputy in Cooper County, Tennessee, was a lifelong goal, and one he'd never take for granted.

But that didn't mean it didn't have its faults.

Living in a small town with a low crime rate was the dream, but sometimes that made for a slow-ass night. Tonight was one of those nights. Not one call from dispatch or even a reckless driver who needed pulled over. So he drove a route that kept him outside of the city limits and patrolling areas where people found themselves once the sun set and businesses closed.

The county hospital was one of those places.

Fidgeting with the radio, he kept a low hum of country music on to keep his mind engaged and turned toward the emergency room. This would be his second loop on the north side of Water's Edge. Once he headed back toward town, he'd stop somewhere to stretch his legs and maybe grab a cup of coffee to push him through the rest of his shift.

He turned into the parking lot and a set of flashing head-lights at the back caught his attention. Probably an employee walking to their vehicle. Plenty of light shone down from the lamp posts strategically placed around the lot, but he might as well swing around to make sure whoever it was got home safely.

An ear-splitting scream made him push the gas pedal to the floor and shot adrenaline through his veins. He sped forward, screeching to a stop in front of a man with a black ski mask over his face struggling to keep a woman pressed against his chest.

Cody jumped out of the vehicle with his hand on the butt of his weapon. As much as he wanted to tackle the guy to the ground, he had no idea what he'd stumbled across. He had to keep a cool head and steady hand.

The woman thrashed against her captor. Her sandy blond hair whipped in front of her face.

The man stiffened, lifted his knife in the air, and waved it before putting it back against the woman's side. "Stay away. Don't make me do anything to hurt her."

If the situation wasn't so terrifying, Cody would laugh at the absurdity of the man's statement. If he didn't want to hurt anyone, he wouldn't have a knife to some woman in the ER parking lot.

Keeping one hand on the weapon, Cody lifted his other palm. "Why don't you just let her go? I mean, what are your options, buddy?"

The wind died down and the curtain of hair around the woman's face dropped. Katherine Milton stared back at him with wide, terrified brown eyes.

His stomach muscles tightened.

He and Katherine weren't exactly friends, but they'd both

grown up in Water's Edge. Her father the sheriff, his family often behind bars. He worked hard to earn a good reputation as a sheriff's deputy, erasing any preconceptions heaped on his shoulders with a father and brother who didn't know how to stay on the right side of the law.

But some people refused to see him for more than his last name. Katherine was one of them.

"Why don't you mind your business?" the man spat out, yanking Cody back to the very dangerous moment.

Cody kept his gaze away from Katherine and his eyes locked on the ominous darkness of the holes around the man's eyes. "You and I both know I can't do that. I'm here until this ends, and soon so will the backup I called the second I saw you out here. That means it's you and one knife against soon-to-be three sheriff's deputies and our weapons. I don't really like your odds, so it'd be a safer bet to just finish this now without hurting anyone."

The man snorted. "Smooth talker. Think you can just show up and save the day."

Cody shrugged. "Just trying to do my job."

Katherine moved her hand slowly toward her jacket pocket.

Cody bit back the urge to tell her to stop moving. He didn't want her captor to sense anything was happening but also cringed at the thought of her gaining more of the man's wrath and getting stuck with a knife before Cody had a chance to stop him.

Katherine might not be his favorite person, but he knew she had a little boy at home who'd already lost one parent. He didn't need to lose another.

"Your job? That's a joke in this town. Guilty people walking around free as a bird while the innocent suffer. You should be ashamed to wear that badge."

Cody opened his mouth to respond but the loud blast of a

car alarm screeched through the night sky. The headlights of Katherine's car blinked on and off, on and off.

Startled, the man's arm loosened around Katherine's neck.

She lunged forward.

Cody lifted his gun to get off a shot, but the man shoved Katherine hard in the middle of the back.

She stumbled toward the pavement.

Shifting gears, Cody maneuvered his body to land under Katherine's. The hard pavement scraped against his side as her soft, lean body fell in his lap.

"You okay?" he asked, his arms wrapping around her on instinct. He peered around her and caught sight of the man disappearing into the patch of woods that surrounded the edge of the parking lot.

Her whole body shivered, and she rested her head on his shoulder for a beat. "I...I don't know. I can't believe that just happened."

He held her tighter, the shock in her system clear to him. He had to call in the incident, but right now, he just wanted her to know she was safe. "Did he hurt you?"

She shook her head. "Just scared the crap out of me."

He snorted out a humorless laugh. "Me, too."

She pulled away and stared at him with those big brown eyes. "Really?"

"You think facing down a masked man holding a beautiful woman hostage in a dark parking lot is an everyday thing for me?"

She blinked up at him and the tremors left her body.

Shit. He'd called her beautiful and admitted to being scared while on the job. Probably something her ex-sheriff dad and two brothers never admitted.

Even if they were.

Owen and Tommy might have been sheriff's deputies for years—Owen now serving as the county sheriff—but every man and woman behind a badge understood the fear that came along with doing their job.

"I guess I never really thought about that," Kathrine said, answering the question that lingered between them. She cleared her throat and pushed to her feet. "Thank you."

He stood and winced at the burning sensation of raw skin on his side. "I didn't do much. You took a risk setting off that alarm. But you might want to turn it off now."

"Oh geez." She fumbled to retrieve her keys and shut off the alarm. "Where's your backup?"

"I lied. I didn't call anyone." He cracked a small smile. "Looks like we both made some risky decisions, but for now let's head into the hospital so I can get your statement."

She blew out a long breath. "Yeah. Let's get that done fast. I need to get home. My dad's waiting up for me. He's going to freak out."

He kept his mouth shut as he walked her inside the emergency room. Her dad wasn't the only one who'd be upset by tonight's attack. The whole damn sheriff's department would be in an uproar, and he'd found himself directly in the middle of the upcoming shitstorm.

2

Fear burrowed into Katherine like a tick. She recalled all the tricks her therapist had taught her over the past year to keep her emotions from swallowing her whole. She couldn't get sucked into anything that would take her away from her number one focus.

Getting home safely to Ollie.

She sat in the break room, a space she'd been in a brief ten minutes before. She'd been tired and overwhelmed and on the brink of insanity, but that was her new normal. Now, her knee bounced up and down and her heart rate had to be triple it's normal speed.

"Katherine?"

Cody Hogan's gentle voice guided her back to the conversation. He sat in a chair across from her with a small notebook on the white table, a pen in hand.

"I'm sorry. I spaced out for a second. Did you ask me another question?"

He offered her a patient smile. "Did the man who attacked you look or sound familiar?"

She shook her head and circled her hands around the

paper cup in front of her. Coffee was the last thing she'd needed earlier, but now she sipped the hot liquid like it was the answer to her prayers.

"Did he say anything to you?"

"Just not to do anything stupid." The reminder of his warm breath on her neck as he spoke shot bile up her throat.

Cody's smile morphed into a lopsided smirk that highlighted his chiseled jawline and made weird things happen to her stomach. "It's a good thing you didn't listen."

She dropped her gaze to her cup. What the hell was wrong with her? Must be the flood of emotions whipping around inside of her because any kind of reaction to the man sitting in front of her was completely inappropriate.

Especially when that man was former bad boy Cody Hogan.

"I've never liked people telling me what to do." She gave a casual shrug and tightened her mouth in a firm line so she wouldn't match his smile with a grin of her own.

The door to the break room banged open and both of her brothers barged inside. Tommy wore his well pressed deputy uniform and his face was clean-shaven while Owen sported jeans and a T-shirt, dark scruff covering his face.

Owen marched straight to her and pulled her into a fierce hug. "Holy shit, are you okay?"

She melted against him, grateful for his presence. "I'm fine, just a little shaken."

"Did he hurt you?" The hard edge of Tommy's voice would have knocked her off balance, but she understood his fear.

Hell, their family had been dealt their fair share of hard knocks. First with losing their mother to a hit and run driver when they were younger, then Theo's accident the year before. Her and her siblings knew how precious life was and how quickly it could be taken away.

She pulled away from Owen and squeezed Tommy's arm.

"No, he didn't hurt me. Luckily Cody showed up in time to scare him off before things took a turn for the worse."

Standing, Cody nodded. "Evening."

"You get a good look at this asshole?" Owen barked.

"Not enough for an ID," Cody said. "He was wearing a ski mask, hiding any distinguishing facial features. He was about four inches taller than Katherine, solid build, but couldn't gauge a good read on what was under his jacket. He ran off after shoving Katherine."

Tommy clenched his jaw. "You said you weren't hurt."

"I wasn't," she said. "Cody caught me before I hit the ground." The memory of his hard body under hers and the way he'd wrapped her in his strong arms brought heat clashing against her cheeks. She really had to get a grip, especially in front of her brothers.

"I wanted to go after the attacker but thought it best to stay with Katherine. By the time I was able to get off the pavement, he was long gone. Disappeared into the woods."

"Have you checked the security footage yet?" Owen asked.

"Not yet," Cody said.

"And why the hell not?" Owen asked.

"Katherine just finished her statement. I wanted to get that first so she could get home to her son." Not an ounce of disrespect dripped from Cody's words, but it was clear he wouldn't stand for being pushed around by anyone.

Not even his boss.

The color drained from Owen's face, and he scrubbed a palm over his whiskers. "Christ. Ollie. Yeah, you should get home, Katherine. Tommy, can you take her?"

If she wasn't sure of her brother's good intentions, she would have bristled at the suggestion. "That's very sweet, but I have my car in the lot. I can drive myself."

"I'll walk you to your car then follow you home." Tommy

folded his arms over his broad chest as if his word were law, no discussion needed.

She bit back the frustration that came with having two overprotective brothers. Even before Theo's death, both Owen and Tommy always thought they knew what was best for her. Always hovered a little too close.

But they'd learned the hard way over and over again that bad things still happened, no matter how much was done to keep it away.

Not wanting to upset Tommy, she rested a hand on his arm. "I'll take the escort across the parking lot but there's no need to follow me home."

Cody frowned, and she couldn't help but wonder what went through his mind watching her and her siblings negotiate. He had siblings of his own, but it was no secret they preferred to use their fists over their words.

Clearing his throat, he gained all their attention. "This guy's still out there, Katherine. We don't know if it was a targeted attack or a case of you being in the wrong place at the wrong time. It might be safer for Tommy to make sure you get inside your home without further incident, and that no one follows you through town to your house. No need bringing more danger to your doorstep."

"I never thought about it like that," she said, the fear from earlier coming back in full force.

A pulse in Cody's jaw made her think he wanted to say more—do more—but he stood quietly, his blue eyes intense and focused.

"So a full escort it is," Tommy said, adding a false note of enthusiasm to his voice.

She appreciated the effort, especially since Tommy was usually the more jovial of the brothers, but a weird flash of disappointment had her focusing way too much on Cody.

Still silent.

She forced her attention to Tommy. "Sounds good. Thanks."

She might not like the idea of her little brother acting as her babysitter for the moment, but it was the smartest move. Besides, she didn't want to waste time arguing. Ollie waited for her at home, and she needed to get the hell away from Cody and whatever weird feelings he stirred in the pit of her stomach.

Because if being held captive by a dangerous stranger was scary, the idea of feeling anything beyond gratitude for Cody Hogan was downright terrifying.

A KNOT of tension at the back of Cody's neck eased a fraction once Katherine was gone. He may have known her for most of his life, but that didn't mean they were friends. If anything, she'd barely tolerated him in high school, opting to stare past him instead of commenting on his troublesome family.

Which, in a way, had been worse.

Any attention from her would have been better than none. But that was years ago. He'd learned a long time ago that a woman like Katherine Wells—now Milton—was never meant for him. Earning the respect of her father and brothers better served him as he carved out a spot for himself in the sheriff's department.

And now one of those brothers was his boss and stood in front of him with a look of concern rippling across his forehead.

Owen stared at the closed door, as if trying to see beyond the barrier to watch his sister make it home in one piece.

Cody understood the other man's worry but didn't want to stand around twiddling his thumbs. "Now that I have Katherine's statement, I'm going to take a look at the security footage. I already asked the guard to set it up. He said to come to his office when I was ready."

"Okay." Owen blew out a long breath and scrubbed a palm down his face. "I'll come with you. This is an all hands-on deck situation. Katherine doesn't need to worry about some asshat coming after her again. Especially after everything she's been through."

He could argue no one in Cooper County should have to worry about being attacked regardless of who they were, but he was smart enough to keep that comment to himself. Besides, he agreed. The more deputies working to track down the man who threatened Katherine, the better.

Without a word, he led the way to the well-lit hallway that wound around the nurses' station to the security office. Even in the administrative area of the hospital, the scents of strong disinfectant and an undertone of sickness stung his nostrils.

He pushed it out of his mind as he knocked twice on the doorframe and peeked his head inside. "You ready for us, Gus?"

"Come on in." Gus, a seventy-something man with a headful of gray hair and a wrinkled uniform that hung on his lanky frame, sat behind a trio of screens at a large desk that took up most of the room. Each screen was split into different quadrants, showing areas of the hospital. The largest screen in the center had a paused scene from the parking lot. "Figured I'd start the tape right before Katherine came outside, just in case we can see anything."

"Good thinking." Owen stepped behind Gus and leaned forward, gaze fixed on the screen.

Cody stood to the side. This was his case, but he wasn't about to have a pissing match with the sheriff about who got the better view. Besides, the only thing that mattered was finding the culprit. He crossed his arms over his chest and kept his eyes on the monitor. "Go ahead."

Gus guided the cursor to the start button then swiveled his chair out of the way.

A few seconds passed before Katherine appeared. Gus chose to display the camera that focused on the area closest to Katherine's vehicle. From this angle, she was almost unrecognizable as she made her way out of the hospital.

At least to most people.

But Cody would recognize her the second she came into view, no matter how far away she was. She had a certain walk, always had. Shoulders straight and chin tilted slightly toward the sky. Her long strides matched her long legs, and she carried a confidence most people never found. Not in a snobbish way, but in a way that let everyone know she was sure of who she was and what she wanted.

And it was sexy as hell.

A flash of movement at the corner of the screen caught his attention and ripped him away from his inappropriate thoughts. "Did you see that?" He pointed at the corner of the screen.

Owen nodded. "Someone's there. Waiting."

A fresh wave of anger tapped his booted toe against the hard floor. "She's walking straight toward him and has no idea. Son of a bitch."

"Must be hiding behind the lamp post. There's a wide cement base that raises a good two feet. Bet he's crouched behind it. Katherine pays attention to her surroundings. No way she'd keep strolling to her car in a dark, empty lot if she saw a man standing there."

"In her statement, she says he came out of nowhere," Cody said.

He kept watching as Katherine got closer, grabbing her keys to unlock her door seconds before the man sprang up and grabbed her from behind.

"I saw her headlights," Cody said, his anger thrashing

around inside him like a tsunami. "That's why I checked the back of the lot." He didn't tear his eyes away from the struggle, but he could feel Owen's fury as clear as if it was his own.

Neither spoke as the video played. By the time the man shoved her, Cody thought he'd burst through his skin.

The man ran away as Cody comforted Katherine. Watching the scene play out brought back a memory of feeling her in his arms, the pulse of desire in his veins at holding her close. Shit. What the hell was wrong with him?

"You did good, Hogan," Owen said. "If you hadn't shown up..."

He didn't have to finish the thought for Cody to understand where his thoughts wandered. "No need to go there, man. Besides, if she hadn't been smart enough to press her panic button, I'm not sure how it would have played out."

"You would have figured out how to get her out of harm's way. Thank you." Owen faced him and clapped a hand on his shoulder. He gave a small squeeze before dropping his arm to his side and spinning toward Gus. "Can you send this footage to the station? I doubt there's more we can get from it, but we'll damn well try."

"No problem," Gus said.

"Cody, you're the lead on this. I don't want to step on toes but be prepared for a lot of extra hands. Tommy and I both will be involved, and if I know my dad, he won't want to sit on the sidelines. No one rests until this bastard's found. Let's head outside and see if anyone's uncovered anything."

He kept what he hoped was a blank expression on his face as he walked beside the sheriff and back outside. He could handle the Wells men—it was their sister he had to keep his distance from.

3

Before Katherine stepped foot on the wide front porch that wrapped around her two-story brick colonial, her dad was out the door. Former county sheriff Mike Wells marched over the sidewalk, blocking her path and meeting her with open arms.

She drew in a deep breath, inhaling the scents of cedar and cigars that would forever remind her of her father. "Is Ollie asleep?"

"Yeah, he's been out like a light for over an hour."

Knowing her son was safe and sound, asleep in his bed, allowed her to melt against her father and release the torrent of emotions clawing at her throat. Tears burst from her eyes as worst-case scenarios of tonight's events assaulted her like shrapnel. Tremors overtook her body. "I could have died. It would have taken seconds for him to jam that knife in me, leaving Ollie all alone."

"Shh, don't think like that. You're fine now. You're home and here to look after that little boy. Besides, with as much family as we have running around this town, Ollie will never be alone."

She cracked a smile and sucked in a shuddering breath.

Growing up in such a small town meant not only having blood relatives around to keep her in line, but a whole community behind her—and now her son.

"You're right," she said, pulling away and wiping her eyes. She'd given herself a moment to fall apart and now it was time to pull herself back together. She couldn't afford to let herself feel every emotion boiling inside her or putting one foot in front of the other would be impossible.

Mike wrapped an arm around her shoulder again. "Let's get you in the house. It's been a long day, and you need some sleep."

A snort of derision shot from her nose. "I have a feeling I won't be getting any of that tonight."

"I'll stay," Mike said. "Set up in the living room and keep an eye on things so you don't have to worry."

More tears stung the backs of her eyes. She stepped inside her home and tossed her keys in the little dish on the table nestled against the wall in the entryway. "You've been here for hours. No need to stay any longer. I'm a grown woman. I can handle things."

"No one says you can't, but that doesn't mean you should have to do it alone. How about some tea?"

She started to argue but her father dipped down the hall to the kitchen before she could say a word.

Sighing, she shrugged out of her jacket and hung it in the entryway closet. As grateful as she was, she didn't need all the men in her life swooping in to help. She could take care of herself, even if it was nice to know she had support behind her.

Support from her brother when he escorted her home, support from her father who refused to leave her on her own, support from Cody Hogan who'd showed up and saved her.

The memory of the way his arms fit around her hit her square in the chest. Heat climbed the back of her neck. He'd held her so gently yet with so much strength. His blue eyes

showcasing his emotions in a way she'd never experienced—
like they could have an entire conversation without a single
word. The well-trimmed dark beard added to the hint of
danger that clung to him since he'd been a teenager, his short-
cropped hair just messy enough to make her want to run her
fingers through it.

A wave of guilt crashed against her so hard, she braced her
hand on the wall to keep upright. Maybe she should skip the
tea and head straight to bed because she clearly needed the
rest. Fear that she'd lay in bed to only find herself dreaming of
Cody guided her feet to the kitchen.

Her dad filled the kettle and set it on the gas stove. Her
favorite cream-colored mug that read "Nurses Call the Shots,"
scrawled in large red letters, waited for her at her normal place
at the farmhouse table.

A cup of coffee across from it.

She fought her instinct to roll her eyes. Her dad had no
intentions of sleeping tonight, even though the state-of-the-art
security system would alert her if anyone came around.

The whistle sounded, and Mike lifted the navy blue kettle
and carried it to her cup, pouring hot water over the tea bags.
She sat and circled her hands around the warm mug.

Normally, this time of the night she loved sitting in her
quiet kitchen. The lights were dimmed, creating a glow that
softened the white marble countertops. The island was free of
clutter and the dinner dishes all put away. She'd spent hours
toiling over the perfect subway tile to splash along the back-
board and the right shade of gray for the cabinets.

This was the heart of her home, the place her family gathered for meals and to discuss their day. Where the scents of
countless meals mingled with the lemony smell of the diffuser
plugged in next to the sink.

But that wasn't true. Not anymore. Now she realized the
heart of her home had rested in the people who lived there.

And part of that heart had been ripped away and buried in the ground outside of town.

Replacing the kettle, Mike settled into his chair and took a sip of coffee. "Wanna talk about it? Sometimes it helps."

"Will it turn back time and make it so none of this happened?"

A sadness she'd witnessed far too often in her father turned down the corners of Mike's mouth. "I wish it did, honey. But we both know nothing can take away the pain or fear or whatever else that comes along with a shitty situation. We just got to find a way to get through the bad things, knowing better times wait ahead."

She sipped her tea, debating what to say. She had no delusion that talking to her dad would actually help her, but he would get the information sooner or later. Better to get the details from her than making him wait to call Owen.

Pulling in a deep breath, she steadied her nerves and unpacked the trauma she'd just experienced.

Mike sat still and took in every word, his expression morphing from anger to fear to something else she couldn't quite put her finger on. When she finished, she took another sip of the chamomile to soothe her dry throat.

The wheels spinning in Mike's mind were clear in his laser-focused stare. "And you have no idea who this guy was?"

She shook her head. "Nothing about him was familiar. His voice, his scent, the little I saw."

"The crack he made to Cody about law enforcement is the key," Mike said, scratching his jaw.

Frowning, she pulled back the words her attacker had spat at Cody. "He definitely had a problem with authority. Called Cody's job a joke. Could this guy have ambushed me because of my connection to you, Tommy, and Owen?"

Growing up, she'd been painfully aware that people sometimes treated her differently because her father was the sheriff, but she'd never felt targeted because of it. Could someone harbor enough resentment for her family that they'd attack her? Wanting her to be the payback for something that she'd had no control over?

Mike worked his jaw back and forth. "It's possible. I'll call Owen. No way I'm sitting on the sidelines on this one. Cody proved himself tonight, and I won't be a pain in his ass, but I want to be aware of everything that's going on. Do whatever I can to lend a hand until this guy's caught."

She appreciated her dad's insistence on helping, but deep down she understood Mike Wells would still be the county's beloved sheriff if it wasn't for her and the nasty curveball life had thrown her. Law enforcement was in his blood, and now he had one more chance to use his skills to find whoever the hell had attacked her.

CODY STEADIED the medical kit on the sink of the sheriff department's bathroom. He opened the box and found what he needed. Hissing out a breath, he dabbed disinfectant on the raw skin snaking up his side then covered it with a bandage. He hadn't had a chance to clean it out since he'd fallen on the asphalt after catching Katherine in his arms.

Gritting his teeth, he shoved the memory from his mind. His reaction to her had been quick and unavoidable. Something he had as much control over as he did the time the sun rose above the mountains.

At least the sunrise created an explosion of oranges and pinks in the morning sky, bringing with it a little hope for a better day ahead. He didn't want to let his mind dwell on what his reaction to Katherine meant.

Nothing good, that's for sure.

With his scratch taken care of, he lowered his shirt and stepped back out into the busy hive of the sheriff's station.

Deputy Heath Sterling stood in front of the vending machine and fed loose change into the slot before making his selection. He glanced his way with raised brows. "Can I get you anything?"

He blew out a breath and shook his head. "Nah. I'm going to check in with Owen then head home to try and catch an hour or two of sleep."

Frowning, Heath glanced at his watch. "Weren't you off shift a while ago?"

He nodded and shoved a hand through his hair. "Too much adrenaline to call it quits."

Heath's expression twisted into a combination of fury and sympathy. "I heard what happened. I can't believe there's been no other sighting of the man who attacked Katherine. Sounds like he disappeared into a cloud of smoke."

"Which means this wasn't a random attack."

"What do you mean?"

Deciding the chocolate bar in vending looked too good to pass up, he slipped a dollar out of his wallet and into the machine.

Heath stepped to the side to give him space to grab his snack.

He peeled back the wrapper and took a bite of the rich dessert before focusing back on Heath's question. "Looking at the security footage, it was clear the man waited to ambush Katherine. If he got away as quickly as he did, he had a clear idea of where to go and how to cover his tracks. If this was a random attack of a woman alone in a dark lot, chances are higher we would've caught him by now."

Heath blew into the paper cup in his hand before taking a sip. "Makes sense. He made a plan, executed it, just didn't claim the prize he wanted. The question is, why Katherine?"

That's the thought that had plagued him every minute since he'd stumbled across her in a madman's clutches, frightened for her life.

"Hogan. Got a minute?" Owen marched to his side, bags heavy under his eyes.

"Sure. What's up?"

"My dad just showed up. He wants to talk to you. I know you've put in extra time already, and my dad isn't anyone to you but your old boss, but it'd mean a lot to all of us if you sat down with him."

He dipped his chin. "No problem."

"Thanks. I'll tell him to make it quick. He's in my office."

Taking another quick bite of the candy bar, Cody followed through the maze of halls to the sheriff's office. At one point, the idea of sitting and speaking with Mike Wells had scared the hell out of him. He'd been young and so consumed with stepping away from the dark cloud of his family's name, he couldn't fathom a man like Sheriff Wells seeing him as anything more than a speck of dirt under his boot.

But Sheriff Wells was a fair and honest man. Quick to give him a chance to earn his spot and reputation as a deputy. He'd always be grateful that the Hogan name hadn't dragged him down the river like it had the rest of his family.

Even if his brother and father had tried their hardest to convince Cody to follow the family way. Especially when they'd hoped having connections on the inside could grease more than a few wheels.

A ridiculous notion he was quick to squash.

Turning into the doorway, he spotted Mike sitting behind Owen's desk—looking as though he'd never left his position to his son.

Sighing, Owen gave a little shake of his head and closed the door. "Really, Dad? You couldn't take the visitor's seat?"

Mike guffawed. "Where we all sit is the least of your worries right now, don't you think?"

Owen didn't respond, just dropped down into one of two bucket chairs across the desk.

Cody remained on his feet. He didn't plan to stay long and wanted a quick exit in case the two men continued to bicker. The Wells men usually got along, but when patience was thin and emotions high, they had a tendency to take it out on one another.

"Hogan, I wanted to personally thank you for saving Katherine. I saw the tape. If you hadn't shown up, things could have ended very differently." He coughed, as though hiding the dip in his voice at the thought of an outcome none of them wanted to imagine.

"No need to thank me, sir. I was just doing my job."

Mike held up a hand. "You have my gratitude whether you want it or not. I spoke with Katherine, actually just left her place after crashing there for the night, and she told me exactly what happened. I'm not here to make you rehash more details, or to throw my weight around when I have no claim to this investigation. But I would like to be involved however possible. I want to help find this bastard, and I want you to know I'm at your disposal."

He blinked at the turn the conversation had taken. He'd been warned Mike would want a hand in things, which made perfect sense. Having his old boss offer to do Cody's bidding wasn't exactly what he saw coming.

"Owen and I've spoken and I'm aware this is a high-priority case. Not only is Katherine the target, but a violent and dangerous man is at large. I don't care who's in charge or calling the shots as long as we find this guy and put him in a jailcell where he belongs."

A spark of appreciation lit Mike's blue eyes. "I like the way you think. I've also been told you've been on the clock for way too long. You heading home?"

"Was about to, sir."

"Do that, and when you get back to the station, we'll go over where things stand. Until then, I'll work with Owen and Tommy. That okay with you?"

"Yes, sir."

"Good."

He took a step toward the door then hesitated. "How's Katherine?"

Owen glanced over his shoulder and furrowed his brow while Mike leaned forward and rested his elbows on the edge of the desk.

Shit.

He shouldn't have asked. Shouldn't have let his professionalism slip enough to let his personal feelings shine through.

"I just mean, she had a rough night. I hope she got some sleep and feels a little better this morning." Sweat coated his palms, and he fought every instinct not to wipe them on the sides of his pants.

"She's okay," Mike said. "She's strong and knows how to fight back when life knocks her down."

The knot in his gut loosened at the news and he nodded his goodbye before disappearing out the door, leaving Katherine's family staring after him.

4

A little bit of the tension wrapped around Katherine's neck loosened as she stepped into Safe Haven's Women Shelter. After a restless night, she'd woken before Ollie and cooked him a breakfast fit for a little prince— French toast, eggs, bacon, and fresh fruit—then convinced him to head to the shelter.

Not like he needed much convincing.

She'd called ahead and found out Elsie would be at the makeshift store inside the shelter today, her sidekick Jimmy with her as usual. Since the two boys were around the same age, Ollie had perked up at the suggestion of spending time with his buddy.

Which was great since the hike she'd considered was now out of the question. Without knowing the reason behind her attack the night before, she wasn't comfortable being alone with her son in the woods.

After hanging their jackets on the hook by the front door, she followed the sound of voices past the kitchen and to the store Elsie ran for the women who found themselves at the shelter—all the merchandise free for women in need.

Elsie sat on a stool behind the glass counter at the back of the space while Mrs. Collins bustled around the room, looking at clothes and straightening trinkets on display.

A woman Katherine had never seen stuck close to Mrs. Collins, a little girl propped on her hip. The purple bruise around her eye told Katherine she was one of the new guests Jenna had mentioned.

Jimmy sat in the corner with a book. He glanced up when they stepped foot over the threshold as if sensing their presence. "Ollie!" He jumped to his feet and darted across the room.

The woman with Mrs. Collins winced and the baby whimpered.

Anger flared to life inside Katherine. She'd witnessed that reaction countless times inside these walls and it never got easier to stomach.

Mrs. Collins rested a reassuring hand on the woman's arm. "Beth, this is Katherine and her son Ollie. She's a nurse and comes to help out when we need another set of hands, or just because she loves to give back. Isn't that right, Katherine?"

She offered a kind smile. "Yep. My son Ollie and I love to hang with our friends. We're like one big happy family."

Ollie scrunched his nose and stared up at her with wide, brown eyes. "Jimmy's my brother?"

Jimmy threw his head back and laughed. "No, silly. But we're *like* brothers, right Aunt Elsie?"

"That's right. You even fight like siblings sometimes."

Jimmy rolled his eyes. "No, we don't. Come on, Ollie. I want to show you my book."

Katherine was eternally grateful to see a glimmer of excitement lighten his steps as he scampered to the corner Jimmy had set up as a reading nook. Two blue beanbags were propped against the wall with a little table on one side. Two cups and a bowl of chips rested on the stand.

Beth offered a small wave then quieted the baby before returning her focus to Mrs. Collins.

"He's been very excited for you guys to get here," Elsie said. "How are you this morning?"

The low timber of her voice told Katherine the gossip mill had been on full blast this morning. She groaned, wishing that for once, her small town wouldn't use everyone's trauma as breakfast conversation.

"How did you know?" she asked.

"I watched Amelia for Tommy and Sadie. He wasn't supposed to go in until this morning, but once he heard what happened, he called and asked if he could drop Amelia at my place. Sadie was already working a night shift. He gave me a quick rundown, mostly because he was so flustered and upset. He didn't mean to gossip."

Sighing, Katherine settled on the backless stool at the side of the counter. "That was nice of you to watch Amelia," she said, wanting a few minutes to figure out a response to her original question.

Elsie shrugged. "It's what we do."

The simplicity of her statement touched Katherine, because she'd found out the hard way this year how true those words were. Time and time again the men and women she'd met through the shelter had stepped up for her and Ollie. Determined to help in any way they could.

Something she hoped Beth and her daughter discovered during their stay, no matter how long that was.

"So you're okay?" Elsie asked. "You don't have to talk about it. You've just been through a lot lately, and it sucks this happened. I'm here if you need me, and if you want to talk. Or not. Maybe it'd be better to just drink." She hoisted her glass of water in the air and wiggled her eyebrows.

Katherine laughed, something a few short hours ago she

wasn't sure was possible. "As long as it's water, I'll drink with you. Anything stronger might knock me on my ass. A place I can't afford to be."

Elsie grinned. "I understand that."

Katherine glanced at Ollie to make sure he wasn't listening. Since Theo's death, he tended to tune into her conversations more than he had before. As if he wanted constant reassurance that nothing else would happen to wreck his world. She hadn't told him about the attack last night, and she didn't plan to.

Once she was confident his focus was strictly on Jimmy and the book in his lap, she considered the best way to express the myriad of emotions ping-ponging inside of her. "I'm rattled. I laid in bed all night and replayed the moment that man's arm went around my neck over and over. I was raised to be aware of my surroundings, yet I was completely caught off guard. That scares the crap out of me. In an instant, Ollie could have been an orphan." The last word wedged in her throat and made it hard to breathe. Unshed tears hovered above her lashes, and she blinked to keep them from falling.

Elsie reached for her hand and squeezed. "Oh, honey. I'm so sorry. I can't say I know exactly how you feel, but I understand being scared and at the mercy of someone else's twisted games. Hopefully whoever this guy is will be caught soon and you won't have to worry that he'll come back to hurt you."

A shudder ripped down her spine, shaking her shoulders. "I don't think I'll ever stop worrying."

Elsie gave her hand another squeeze. "You're a mom. Moms aren't allowed to stop worrying."

Katherine let out a humorless laugh and cast another glance toward Ollie. "Isn't that the truth."

Elsie removed her palm and found a microfiber rag beneath the counter to wipe down the glass top. "Thank God for Cody. Who'd think he would be your knight in shining armor?"

Warmth clashed against Katherine's cheeks. She and Elsie

had grown up in Water's Edge, both aware of the Hogan family and the trouble that often followed them. She'd steered clear of Cody, even though he'd never stepped out of line as far as she knew, but the idea he was the man who'd saved her sent a thrill to her heart that confused the heck out of her.

"Yeah, who'd have thought?" she asked, eager to change the subject to anything else.

Because the thought of any man besides Theo as her knight in shining armor terrified her.

Especially if that man was Cody Hogan.

GRAINS OF SAND clawed at Cody's eyes as he stared at the computer screen. He'd managed to get a couple hours of shut eye, more than enough to push him through the rest of the day. He wasn't due back to the sheriff's station until later, but that didn't mean he couldn't get some work done while home. Besides, he much preferred the comfortable leather chair in his office than the hard one at his desk at the station. Not to mention the coffee was better and he could enjoy the spring breeze floating in through the open window.

Bailey, his oversized Bernedoodle, rested her head on his lap and whined.

"What is it, girl?"

He'd inherited the fluffy dufus dog when his dear old dad was sent to prison again—this time hopefully for good. As far as he was concerned, Bailey was the best thing he'd ever gotten from his father. Even if the mutt was too mouthy for her own good, always interrupting with a bark or a whine to get what she wanted.

Bailey ran in a tight circle then made a beeline for the door.

Needing a break anyway, he stood and followed her into the

attached living room. A pair of French doors in the kitchen led outside.

Bailey jumped up and down in front of the door, her vertical leap enough to impress an NBA player.

"Okay, outside it is." He slipped into his slides and led the way outside. He leaned against the railing of his deck and took in the view he'd never tire of.

Bailey raced down the steps to the fenced-in back yard. She sniffed the perimeter of the yard, squatting to do her business before a squirrel caught her attention and she took off after the brown, furry creature.

Growing up, he couldn't imagine finding a way to escape the trailer park just outside of town where he'd been raised. The dingy, faded walls had caged him in, threatening to crush him. He'd never wanted the life he'd been born into. The empty beer cans stacked on the counter and the constant yelling. Things had been tolerable until his mother died.

Then the real nightmare began.

He hadn't understood how much his mother had protected him. How she'd shielded him from the cruelty of his father and older brother. Without her, he'd struggled to stay under the radar and off the tragic path that led to trouble and jail.

A choice his family didn't understand and often found insulting.

But he'd escaped that world and carved out a small place with the mountains as his neighbors and silence his company.

Well, that was until he got Bailey.

The blast of the doorbell forced his attention back inside. Knowing Bailey couldn't be torn from her hunt, he left her in the yard and headed inside where he found Tommy on his front porch.

"Hey, man. What's up?" He got along with his co-worker, but the two didn't exactly socialize outside of work.

Tommy shoved a hand through his already messy hair.

Dark circles hung under his bloodshot eyes. "Sorry to barge in on you like this. I just...I don't know, dude. I'm having a hard time wrapping my mind around what happened to Katherine. I didn't get a chance to talk to you about it, and I know it's not cool showing up at your house. I guess I just hoped we could talk."

"Uh, sure. Come on in." He stood back to let Tommy in then shut the door behind them. Frantic barking clued him in that Bailey had spied their visitor. "You okay with dogs?"

"Yeah, sure." Tommy sank onto the recliner in the corner of the living room.

Cody crossed over to the kitchen and let in Bailey, who sprinted across the room to Tommy.

Unaware that her giant size wasn't meant for lap-sitting, she hopped onto the chair, her tail wagging like crazy.

Laughing, Tommy shooed the dog to the ground and ran his hand over her fluffy head. "Have yourself a real killer, huh?"

"You have no idea. Bailey, get down." He waited for the dog to settle on the floor, gaze intent on Tommy and tail thumping against the hard wood, before lowering onto the couch. "So what's up?"

"I need to clear my head," Tommy said. "And to be honest, I'm not sure how to do that. Serving as a deputy, I've seen my fair share of scary shit. Hell, even ran into some trouble that could have cost me Sadie. But Sadie's a trained officer and knows how to handle herself. Katherine...that's different. She doesn't deserve any more crap tossed at her feet."

Although he agreed with Tommy, he wasn't sure what that had to do with him. "I get that. She's had a tough year. With any luck, this was a one-time thing."

Concern wrinkled Tommy's brow. "Do you really believe that?"

Sighing, Cody scratched the side of his jaw. He was a straight-shooter, not great at cushioning his words, but he had a feeling Tommy needed more than the hard truth right now. "I want to, but it's difficult to tell right now. There's no real reason to assume Katherine's attacker will come after her again. His anger seemed more targeted toward me and my job than Katherine specifically. Even though we need to get him off the street to make sure he doesn't do something like this—or worse —again, I don' t know why he'd choose to keep going after Katherine."

Tommy bobbed his head up and down as if in agreement. "Yeah. That makes sense. When I left the station, Dad and Owen were looking at recent crimes that could stick out. Something where the wrong person was arrested or notes were made about hostile family members."

Cody couldn't help but laugh.

"Why's that funny?" Tommy asked, frowning.

"Great minds think alike. I was doing the same thing here before you arrived. Looking up old news articles to see if anything sent up a red flag."

"Find anything?"

"A couple stories I found interesting. I saved them and planned to talk to your brother about them when I went in." He glanced at his watch. "My shift's not for another three hours, but I might as well head in early. If we're researching the same shit, it'd be better to bounce things off each other."

Tommy stood, his hand automatically reaching for the top of Bailey's head. "I should tell you not to bother, but I know we'd all appreciate the extra support. Not to mention Owen and I will need to take a break at some point. Sadie's with Amelia, but I can't expect her to stay home while I work twenty-four hours a day. It's just hard not to keep going—keep searching for this asshole."

"Understandable," Cody said. "But there's an entire sheriff's department behind you—behind Katherine."

Tommy sniffed back emotion and nodded. "Thanks, man. For everything. I'll see you back at the office."

Cody walked Tommy to the door and watched him lope down the porch steps and to his cruiser. He hoped he hadn't lied to the man. As much as he wanted to believe Katherine was out of the fire, he couldn't help the nagging feeling in the pit of his stomach telling him the pot had just begun to boil.

5

As always, spending time at the shelter kept Katherine's mind busy and off her problems. While Ollie stayed glued to Jimmy's side, she bopped around where needed—changing bedding, preparing lunches, and chatting with Beth about what brought her to the shelter.

As difficult as it was to keep her emotions from her face, she remained passive as possible while listening to the young woman's struggles.

Slicing a cucumber, Beth sighed and stared out the kitchen window. "The hardest part is worrying about Audrey. Wondering if my mistakes will haunt her for the rest of her life."

Katherine rinsed a head of lettuce in the sink before breaking off leaves for a salad. "All mothers worry about that. I strongly believe as long as we do the best we can and shower our children with love and good intentions, they'll be all right."

"I hope so. But I doubt your son has been dealt as crappy a hand as my daughter." There was no bite in Beth's words, just an exhausted acceptance of a rough life.

The side of Katherine's mouth hitched up. "You'd be surprised."

Beth held the knife over the cucumber and stared at her with wide, brown eyes. "You were abused, too?"

"No," Katherine said, shaking her head. "I was in a wonderful marriage with a man who made the best possible father."

"Told you." Beth went back to her task.

"But that's not the end of our story," Katherine continued. "He died in a car accident a year ago. Someone else's mistake took away half of my heart and left us struggling to accept our new reality. The reason I'm here might be different than yours, but deep down, I need the same community you do. And if you let them, the women here can be there for you just like they have been for me."

A sad smile touched Beth's lips. "I hope so."

She opened her mouth to say more, but Ollie and Jimmy ran into the room with matching grins.

"Mama, Jimmy wants to see my fidget spinner. The shiny blue one Pappy gave me. Can you go get it? Please." Ollie drew out the last word in a desperate plea.

Normally she'd say no and tell the boys to play with something already at the shelter or go outside and enjoy the sun. But it wasn't often Ollie displayed so much excitement, and she had to admit, the fact her eighty-something grandfather had bought a fidget spinner delighted the entire family. Something her grumpy-yet-loveable Pappy pretended to find irritating.

"It sounds really cool, Ms. Katherine," Jimmy added, excitement bouncing him up on his toes.

Beth chuckled. "Looks like they're wanting you to run an errand."

"Sure does." Katherine gave an exaggerated eye roll. "Maybe if they both promise to be very good for the rest of the day and eat all these delicious vegetables we're preparing for lunch, I can grab the toy really quick and bring it back."

Ollie threw his arms around her waist. "Thanks, Mom!"

She savored the affection for a second longer before popping into the storeroom to tell Elsie she'd be right back. Once Elsie assured her that she'd keep an eye on the boys, she slipped into her jacket and snatched her keys from the pocket. She rushed down the porch steps to her SUV and turned on the engine.

Soft music played from the speakers, and she hummed along with the melody. The frazzled state of her nerves evened out from a day giving back, and she settled into the drive from Pine Valley to Water's Edge. With her home on the outside of town, the fifteen-minute drive often went fast. Especially this time of year when the bright colors of spring promised warmer weather.

She drove past the town square, stopping at the red light. A few pedestrians filtered past on the crosswalk. She tapped her fingertip against the steering wheel as she waited, and when the light turned green, she turned right away from town.

The houses grew further apart and the trees more prominent, the wind ruffling the leaves. She cracked her window to let the fresh air inside and turned up the radio. Alone time wasn't something she got often. She might as well enjoy it as much as possible before returning to the shelter.

A quick glance in the rearview mirror showed an old truck closing the distance between them. She kept her speed right at the limit. If some eager beaver had a lead foot, he could pass her. Keeping her hands at ten and two, she fixed her attention straight ahead. The road curved around the mountain, and she couldn't afford to be distracted.

The truck came closer, raising the hairs at the back of her neck. Intuition tingled her gut, and she put a little extra pressure on the gas pedal. The more space she carved out between her and the truck, the more even her heartbeat became.

She darted her gaze between the rearview mirror and the windshield. The truck stayed back, following her into Water's Edge.

Take it easy. Just some random guy in a truck taking the same route. No big deal.

She took the final curve around the bend.

In a flash, the truck was on her bumper. She glanced over her shoulder for a glimpse of the driver, but a hat pulled low over his eyes kept any features hidden. Fear hitched her breath as the space between the two vehicles became almost non-existent.

She increased her speed a little more and found the call button on her steering wheel. She might be overreacting, her paranoia at an all-time high after the night before, but her instincts screamed that something wasn't right.

When the sound dinged through her speakers, she said, "Call the sheriff's department."

The line picked up and ringing overtook the country music on the radio.

"Sheriff's department, this is Anne. How can I help you?"

"Anne, it's Katherine. I'm driving into town, about five miles south of the city limits, and a truck behind me is freaking me out. I'm in a black SUV. Are there any deputies out this way?"

"One second, honey. Let me see what I can do."

Time ticked by slowly. Katherine kept her foot on the gas and focus ahead of her. She didn't have to keep looking back to know the truck was still right behind her. The turn to her house came into view, but she didn't want to lead this guy to her home.

She drove in the opposite direction. She'd take him into town, pass a traffic camera so they could get a better look at the guy's license plate.

A sudden bump against the back of her SUV lurched her vehicle to the side and whipped her body forward. Her seatbelt tightened, biting into her middle. Fear clouded her vision, and she gripped the wheel in her sweat-slicked palms, cranking it back to center.

"Anne," she said, terror clipping her voice. "The truck just hit me."

"Okay, honey. I just spoke with a deputy in the area. Help's on the way. Just hold on."

She took the suggestion to heart, holding on to the steering wheel like it was a lifeline. Her pulse beat against her temples, and she chanced a quick glance in the rearview mirror, catching sight of the truck one more before it slammed into the back of her vehicle. The sound of metal crunching metal scraped along her skin and her front tires bounced on the berm, spinning out of control.

CODY MADE a U-turn on his way to the sheriff's station and headed south of town. The call from dispatch requested a deputy to check out a situation with two drivers headed toward Water's Edge. He had no clue what the issue was beyond a woman upset somebody drove too close to her car, but he'd make sure everything was okay.

Chances were high it was some teenager running late for something and with no regard for others on the road.

To make it quick, he turned on his siren and activated the flashing lights that would clear his path. He sped to the country road that fed into Water's Edge. He spotted the black SUV seconds before the truck behind it rammed into the back and sent it spinning off the road.

The SUV whipped to the side and crashed against the guardrail. The bright yellow metal bent and twisted, straining to keep the vehicle from plummeting into the ravine on the other side.

"Son of a bitch!"

He increased his speed and grabbed the receiver of his communicator. "Found the SUV and there's been an accident. Send an ambulance to County Road 81, a few miles south of Water's Edge. The perp is fleeing in the opposite direction, heading toward Pine Valley. Send deputies, keeping an eye out for a four-door black truck with an extended cab."

As much as he wanted to chase after the dumbass who'd sent the SUV into such a precarious situation, he had to make sure the SUV driver and possible passengers made it out safely. And the way the guardrail had shifted told him he didn't have a lot of time.

Closing the distance between him and the accident, he threw his cruiser in park and jumped outside. He ran to the SUV, sending up a quick prayer whoever was inside wasn't injured and could be easily removed before things got worse.

As he approached the driver's side door, shock threatened to knock all the sense from his brain.

Katherine sat with her hands glued to the steering wheel and wide eyes fixed straight ahead. Her shoulders raised up and down as though releasing her breaths at a rapid rate.

He tapped on her window.

Her body jolted, and she turned her head his way.

Even with the glass between them, he could see the shock holding her hostage. He lifted a palm then pointed to the door handle. He tested the handle, relief flooding over him when the door flew open. "Katherine, are you injured?"

Swallowing hard, she shook her head and tears leaked down her cheeks.

"That's good. Can you unhook your seatbelt so we can get you out of the vehicle? That guardrail is keeping you in place and I'm not sure how much longer it'll hold."

Her hands trembled but stayed locked on the wheel.

The pallor of her face worried the hell out of him. He needed to get her out of the car.

"That's okay," he said, inching closer. "I can help. Is that okay?"

She nodded.

Leaning into the vehicle, he reached around her to release the belt. The scent of lavender and vanilla hit him square in the chest, taking him back to the night before when he'd held her in his arms. He shoved those thoughts out of his brain. Now wasn't the time to dwell on whatever that reaction was. Especially with Katherine yet again needing help out of a potentially dangerous situation.

"I'm going to slip my arm around your back and get you out of the vehicle now." He did just that and gently applied pressure to coax her to move. He could lift her out if needed but that would be a last resort.

His touch must have snapped her out of whatever haze held her captive. She jolted forward, her hand gripping his arm as she jumped out of the seat.

He held her steady. "I got you," he said. "You're safe."

Her body shook and she clung to the front of his uniform, fisting the fabric by his neck in her small hands.

"Let's get you to my cruiser. I have some water."

She kept her grip firm as he guided her to his car.

"I need to get in my car to grab the water," he said.

When she didn't remove her death grip, he covered the back of her hand with his palm and guided it to his side. He opened the passenger side door and found an unopened bottle of water in the console. He handed it to her. "Are you injured?"

Her chin quivered and the tears poured out faster. "I...I'm sore. The truck. It hit me. Pushed me off the road. Just like Theo. I could have—" Sobs stole the rest of her words. She used her free hand to cover her mouth and her face twisted in pure agony.

Unable to stop himself, he pulled her close and wrapped his arms around her. He moved his palm up and down her spine, doing whatever he could to console her. Hell, he'd assumed her reaction was solely based on fear. He hadn't considered the PTSD that'd paralyze her due to her losing her husband in a fatal accident.

She buried her head against the side of his neck and clung to him.

"You're fine. Do you hear me? You made it out of that car without a single scratch."

Pulling back, she sniffed back her tears and locked her gaze on his. "Last night was scary. But this...I *knew* something wasn't right. That the guy behind me wasn't just some random stranger who needed to get somewhere fast. Then when he hit me...all I could think about was Theo and what must have gone through his head that night. What would Ollie do if the same thing happened to me?"

The crack in her voice shredded his heart. He tucked a long piece of hair behind her ear and forced her eyes to meet his. "Don't let your mind circle around the what ifs, or you'll drive yourself crazy."

She nodded and drew in a shuddering breath. "You're right. Thank you."

The sound of a siren broke them apart.

Katherine winced and gingerly touched her fingertips to the side of her neck.

Frowning, he shoved his hand in his pocket to keep from touching her again. "An ambulance will be here soon. They'll check you over. Do you want me to call anyone for you?"

Sighing, she squeezed her eyes shut for a beat. When she opened them again, defeat was clear in her brown hues. "My dad's going to flip. He'll never leave my side after this."

"He's worried about you. That's what dads are for." Not like he'd know. His dad was usually the source of his worrying, not the person looking out for him.

"You're right. He's great, and so are my brothers and grandfather. I'm so appreciative of their help, and after this, that help will be needed. I'm not sure I'll feel safe on my own. There's no way it's a coincidence I've been targeted two days in a row. Don't you think?"

He wished he could lie to her. That he could tell her there was a chance, however slim, that she'd been in the wrong place at the wrong time twice. But she wasn't an idiot, and he wasn't one to lie to protect someone's feelings. Honesty was always best.

"I think someone wants to hurt you, and I'm afraid they won't stop until they get what they want."

6

Katherine sat in the back of the ambulance and stared into the penlight the medic shone in her eye. She clasped her hands in her lap as anxiety danced up her spine. Not because of the madman out to get her, but because Cody was steps away speaking with her family.

"No concussion," Catie, the young medic, said and clicked off the light. "I recommend over-the-counter pain medicine. Maybe some ice to help with soreness. Try and take it easy if you can."

She almost laughed. What single working mother ever had the opportunity to take it easy?

"Thanks, Catie. Am I free to go?"

When Catie gave a little nod, Katherine hopped out of the ambulance and walked over to where the men huddled by Cody's cruiser.

Cody glanced up and his gaze latched on hers. He raised his eyebrows as if asking a silent question.

She offered a small smile, relaxing the wrinkles in his forehead. There it was again. That silent communication. How was that possible? She barely even knew Cody, but there was something about this man that was so easy for her to read—to understand.

Something about him that made her want to know more.

A quiver vibrated deep inside of her. She wanted to explore that reaction, wanted to pull it out and dissect and understand, but now wasn't the time.

Her dad glanced over his shoulder, spying her approach, then quickly strode her way. He gave her a quick hug then took a step back, bracing her biceps in his large hands. "You okay?"

"Yeah, just a little stiff. Nothing too bad."

OWEN JOINED THEM, his frown deeper than the Grand Canyon. "Tommy's out looking for this asshole's vehicle with Heath and a few other deputies. Pine Valley PD is pulling traffic camera footage to see if they can get a visual of the truck or license plate. I'll be in touch with them as soon as we're done here. Is there anything else you can tell us that can help find this guy?"

She shook head then winced. Her injuries may be minimal but the pain in her head pounded against her temples. "I already told you everything I can. He followed me for a while, came up on me quickly, then ran me off the road."

The last thing she wanted to do was replay the whole ordeal again. She'd already told Cody exactly what had happened. Going over it once more wouldn't jar anything else from her memory. Every second of the accident would haunt her for the rest of her life.

"Where's Ollie?" Mike asked.

"At the shelter with Elsie and Jimmy."

Mike blew out a long breath and scrubbed a hand down his face. "Thank God. Your vehicle's totaled. I'll get a tow truck out here, but for now why don't you jump in with me and Owen? We'll drive over to Pine Valley and get Ollie."

Her dad's plan made sense, but something kept her from agreeing.

As if sensing her hesitation, Cody tilted his head to the side and studied her with narrowed eyes. "What's wrong?"

"If I show up with you two in Owen's cruiser, Ollie will know something's wrong. I don't want him learning about this. He's had a hard enough time after Theo's accident. He doesn't need to be told I was in one, too."

"I understand wanting to protect Ollie," Owen said. "But I don't see any other option."

"She can ride with me," Cody said.

"Excuse me?" Mike asked, his voice holding a note of disbelief.

Cody shrugged. "If you go pick up the boy, she can call ahead and tell him you wanted to take him to do something fun. Or if he wants to stay with his buddy, maybe no one needs to head to get him at all. That keeps him busy and protected, out of harm's way while Katherine figures out how to get another vehicle and hopefully nail this son of a bitch before he tries to hurt her again."

The fact Cody had voiced the exact thoughts that circled her mind dropped her jaw.

"That makes sense," Owen said. "What do you want to do, Katherine?"

She nibbled her bottom lip and ran through her options. She wanted Ollie safe, which he would be with her family, but also didn't want to alarm him. He'd been so happy to be with Jimmy. She hated to cut their time together short.

"If he's safe at the shelter, I think it's best to let him stay there. I'll call Elsie and give her a heads-up. She'll make sure everything's locked down. If Cody doesn't mind, I'll take him up on his offer to catch a ride so you two can contact the officers in Pine Valley."

Her father's scowl told her he wasn't sold on her decision,

but she lifted her chin a fraction to show him she wouldn't change her mind. As much as she loved him and everything he'd done for her, the idea of being babysat for the day by him and Owen was suffocating.

"Pappy has that old truck out at his place you can probably borrow," Owen said.

Mike grunted.

She bit back a grin. Her dad and her grandfather might have gotten along better in the past few years, but that didn't mean the two men actually liked each other. She and her brothers had grown accustomed to their bad blood. Their occasional grunts and eye rolls were tame compared to the blowups that often erupted right after her mom had died when she was a teenager.

"I can drive you to your grandfather's," Cody said.

"Can we swing by my place first? I needed to pick up something for Ollie and he'll be disappointed if I don't come back with it."

Cody dipped his chin. "Sure thing."

"All right, looks like we all know what needs done. Dad, let's head out," Owen said. "You get ahold of Tommy and see if he has any information while I call Officer Sawyer. Cody, let me know when Katherine's all settled so we can loop you in."

Mike wrapped her in another hug then turned to Cody. "Keep her safe, Hogan." He marched to Owen's cruiser and climbed into the passenger seat.

Owen sighed. "He's scared shitless."

Katherine let out an indelicate snort. "I know the feeling."

"We've got you, Sis. All of us are determined to catch this guy. I'll be in touch."

Once Owen was behind the steering wheel, she faced Cody and her stomach did a funny little dip. "Thank you."

He lifted a shoulder. "Just doing my job."

The side of her mouth lifted at the casualness in his voice.

"I know what your job is, and you're going above and beyond. I love my family more than anything, but right now I need a little space so I don't have to temper my own reaction to all this just to make them feel better."

"I get it," Cody said. "Glad I can be here for whatever you need."

No matter how innocent his words, they brought something to life inside her that had lain dormant for months.

She needed a ride from him, and that was all. Or at least that's the lie she told herself as she followed him to his car.

THE AIR in Cody's car was thick, the energy practically vibrating. He was painfully aware of every sound Katherine made, every movement. She filled his space with her femininity in a way that made him want to forget about his job for the rest of the day. Made him want to uncover everything he could about the woman he'd steered clear of for most of his life.

"I'm the third house on the left." She flicked her wrist out the window, indicating the large brick colonial.

He couldn't stop the low whistle from coming out of his mouth. "Nice place. Big yard."

"Yeah, it's not fun to mow but Ollie has plenty of room to run around."

Parking in her driveway, he glanced her way with his eyebrows hiked high. "You mow?"

She laughed, the sound like a warm spring rain in his ears. "Is that so hard to believe?"

Shrugging, he opted to step out of his car instead of answering.

She met him at the hood of the cruiser and planted her fists on her hips. "I'm not letting you off the hook. Don't I look like a woman who can handle a mower?"

He swallowed hard. Hell, she looked like the kind of woman who could handle anything he threw her way, but he couldn't say that. "That's not what I meant," he said, searching for a way out of this mess. "I'm sure you have your hands full with taking care of Ollie and working as well as everything else you have going on. Yard work is the last thing you should have to worry about."

Her stance relaxed and a genuine smile touched her lips, deepening her dimples. "Smooth."

Grinning, he followed her up the walkway.

"This won't take long." She pulled out her keys and unlocked the door. When she pushed it open, the screech of an alarm echoed into the afternoon sky. She keyed in numbers to the panel by the door and the screeching stopped.

He took a step inside and studied the panel. "Nice system."

"With family in law enforcement, no way they'd allow anything less than the best. I have to run up to Ollie's room. I'll be back in a second."

He shoved his hands in his pockets and nodded. "Mind if I have a look around the first floor? Just to make sure everything's secure."

She wrapped her arms around her midsection. "Do you think that guy knows where I live?"

He worked his jaw back and forth as he considered his words for a second time. "It's a possibility. He knew you'd be at the hospital last night. He followed you from Pine Valley today. There's no telling how long he's had his eye on you or what patterns of yours he's picked up. You have a great security system in place, so you'd know if he tried to get inside, but it's always a good idea to double check the house. It just takes things slipping through the cracks one time for something bad to happen."

She blew out a long breath. "Makes sense. Do whatever you have to."

He waited for her to make her way up the stairs before turning into the living room at his side. Light poured in from a wall of windows that looked out into the backyard. An over-sized gray sectional covered with decorative pillows faced a fireplace, a large television mounted above it. Framed photos of Katherine, Ollie, and Theo littered the walls and decorated the wooden stands placed beside the furniture.

A picture of the three smiling with the ocean behind them hung on the wall and drew him across the room. Theo threw Ollie in the air while Katherine tilted her head toward the sky in obvious laughter. Pure joy oozed from the photo and tied his insides in a knot.

A happy, thriving family had lived here. A good father and husband ripped away. It wasn't fair.

"What are you looking at?"

The sudden sound of Katherine's voice spun him around. He winced, as though caught doing something he shouldn't. "Sorry."

A sad smile touched her lips and she joined him, her shoulder brushing against his. "That was our last vacation. We took Ollie to Mexico. He loved the beach."

Emotion squeezed his throat. "I'm glad you have that memory. You all look so happy."

She brushed a finger along the front of the frame and sighed. "We were."

"He was a good man."

She faced him, eyes wide. "You knew him?"

He lifted a shoulder. "Not well. I mean, we all went to school together, remember?"

She winced. "Yeah. I guess I forget that sometimes. It was a lifetime ago."

"It was, but I remember it all too well. Theo," he said, dipping his head toward the grinning man. "Was always nice to me. Even when most people in this town treated me like a criminal, he never judged me based on the actions of my family. Never looked down his nose at me because I lived on the wrong side of town or sometimes wore the same shirt three times a week because I didn't have anything else to put on. Our paths didn't cross much in recent years, but when they did, he always had a kind word. I liked him."

Unshed tears glimmered in her eyes. "That sounds like Theo. Such a good man. Thank you for sharing that."

Seeing the emotion twisting her beautiful face gutted him. "I didn't mean to make you cry."

She dashed away the tears. "No, they aren't sad tears. It's just...it's hard to explain. Talking about Theo always brings a rush of feelings, but it's also nice. Like he's not forgotten. Ollie and I talk about him all the time, but that's mostly me reliving memories so Ollie won't forget his dad. But other people, they walk around me on eggshells when his name comes up. As though they'll accidently remind me that I miss him. That pain never goes away, but discussing him with others helps me to focus on the positive things he left behind."

A moment of silence passed between them before Katherine rested a hand on his arm. "Sorry I wasn't more like him."

His skin tingled from her touch. He frowned down at her. "What do you mean?"

"I kept my distance from you. I judged you because of your family when I shouldn't have. You're a good man, and I'm sure you were probably just as great of a teenager. I didn't give you a chance. That was pretty shitty of me."

Her words constricted his throat, but he kept his expression as passive as possible. He didn't want her to know how much it meant that she recognized she'd placed a label on him he'd fought his entire life to rip off. "Teenage girls aren't exactly known for their kindness."

She snorted out a laugh. "True, but I could have been better. I will be better."

Narrowing his eyes, he glanced down at her upturned nose and the tight set of her pretty pink lips. God, he'd do anything to taste her, to find out what her mouth felt like on his.

No, he had to erase that thought from his mind right now. She might have acknowledged she hadn't treated him the best in high school but that didn't mean she wanted anything beyond friendship as adults. Hell, even friendship might be more than she intended. She was a victim who needed protecting, not a woman for him to pine after.

He'd finish double checking her security then drop her at her grandfather's. Then he'd find the asshole after her so she could get on with her life and he could forget that a simple touch from Katherine Milton had set his entire body on fire.

atherine lifted a hand to knock on her grandfather's door then stopped, facing Cody. There really was no reason for Cody to walk her to the house, but a thrill had shot through her when he'd hurried around to open her car door.

Plus, she didn't want him to leave. Spending time with him today was unexpected, but there was something about him that soothed her—settled her in a way that made her forget her world had been turned upside down again.

"I should warn you about my grandfather," she said. "He's a little grumpy."

Scrunching his nose, Cody scratched the back of his neck. "I grew up with a criminal for a father and world's biggest bully for a brother. I think I can handle your grandpa."

"All right, I tried to warn you." She pounded her fist on the door, pasted a smile on her face, and waited for the show to start.

The door swung open, and her sister-in-law Marie appeared on the other side. Her eyes widened in surprise. "Hey! Wasn't expecting you. Come on in."

"Your grandpa looks downright terrifying," Cody said on a laugh.

Marie chuckled and smoothed a piece of dark, curly hair away from her face. "You don't know the half of it." She waited for the two to enter before locking up and following them into the house.

Katherine glanced over her shoulder. "Is he in the kitchen?"

A low grumble from the other room answered her question, and she led the way through the family room to the kitchen.

Pappy stood with his hands fisted on his hips in front of a giggling toddler in a highchair.

Nora, Marie and Owen's daughter, slapped a plastic spoon against the tray of her seat and splattered some kind of green goo all around.

"I told your mother you don't like those damn avocados, but she won't listen to me," Pappy huffed under his breath. "No one ever does."

"Language, Pappy," Katherine said before placing a kiss on his shrunken cheek. "Owen won't be thrilled to hear his little princess speaking like that. Isn't that right, Nora?" She swiped a napkin from the table and wiped the goo from Nora's cheeks before kissing her as well.

"Oh, pish posh. Ain't no one cares how this little one talks as long as she's saying something." Pappy waved a hand in the air then sank down in one of the four chairs at the table, his back facing the wall. He aimed his gaze at Cody and crossed his arms over his chest. "Who the hell are you?"

"Cody Hogan, sir. Just bringing Katherine by."

"Cody, this is my grandfather, Lewis Sinclair," Katherine said.

Pappy ignored the introduction. "And why can't she bring herself? She's a grown-ass woman. Don't need the likes of you hanging out and driving her around town. Dammit girl, you know I don't like strangers. Bad enough I have to put up with family."

Marie chuckled and brought Pappy a cup of coffee. She smoothed the thin gray hairs on the top of his mostly bald head. "We all know that bark is all you've got, and you love us as much as we love you. Now be nice."

"Umph. Being told what to do in my own house. It's a damn shame."

Grinning, Katherine rolled her eyes. "Cody brought me by because I'm having issues with my car and need to borrow the old truck you keep in the garage. Is that okay?"

Straightening, Marie frowned but she didn't say anything. She didn't have to. Concern poured off her in waves. Clearly Owen had let his wife know what had happened.

As if sensing the tension, Pappy tapped the top of his finger against the tabletop. "What happened to your car?"

Katherine sighed. As much as she didn't want to get into the details, lying wasn't an option. Pappy would find out soon enough, and he'd be even pissier if she hid the truth. "I was in an accident."

All the color leeched from Pappy's face, but he kept his expression a hard mask. "You at fault for this accident?"

"No."

A vein ticked at Pappy's temple. "Hit and run?"

The question broke her heart. Her mother had been killed in a hit and run accident years ago, upturning Pappy's—and everyone's—life. He was never the same after losing his only child. Even though justice had finally been served, it still didn't lessen the pain of losing her mother.

"Kind of," she said, then uttered a silent prayer he'd leave it at that.

"What the hell does that mean?"

Prayer unanswered.

"Someone hit the back of Katherine's SUV, sending her off

the side of the road and into a guardrail," Cody said. "Her vehicle's totaled. Deputies are searching for the man responsible."

Pappy worked his jaw back and forth then took a sip of coffee. He kept his gaze fixed on Cody, as if trying to read every thought in his head. "You're a deputy. Why aren't you looking for this guy? Seems an important thing to keep a jackass like that off the road."

The side of Cody's mouth lifted. "Agreed. But Katherine needed a ride. Hated to leave her stranded on the side of the road, waiting for a tow truck."

"Can't say I can blame you for that," Pappy said. "Go ahead, girl. Grab the keys from the drawer. That old thing might need some gas, maybe an oil change. Been a while since anyone's driven it."

She bit back a groan. As much as she appreciated the free ride while she secured something better to drive, she didn't want to spend time upkeeping the hunk of junk.

"I can do that," Cody said.

One gray, bushy eyebrow hooked high on Pappy's wrinkled brow. "Excuse me?"

Cody shrugged. "I can change the oil. Do you have what I'd need in the garage, or should I run into town and grab it?"

"You don't have to do that," Katherine said. "You've already done too much."

"Nonsense." Pappy took another swig from his mug. "Boy says he can change the oil, let him change the oil. I've got every-thing here."

Nora pounded her fists on the highchair, reclaiming the attention. "No cados. More nanas pwease." Her adorable voice smothered all the tension in the room.

Cody snatched a banana from the bowl on the counter and peeled it. "Does she need it sliced?"

Marie darted her gaze between Katherine and Cody,

amusement clear in her dark eyes. "Umm, you can just break off chunks for her if you want."

"Let me wash my hands first." He rounded the Formica peninsula that jutted out from the wall then scrubbed his hands in the kitchen sink.

"Wow," Marie mouthed, her dramatic expression lifting every muscle in her face.

"Stop it," Katherine mouthed back. The last thing she needed was Cody spinning around and catching her and her sister-in-law in a secret conversation about him.

Pappy clicked his tongue. "My house used to be so damn quiet."

Cody returned and sectioned off the banana, placing the pieces on the tray for Nora.

She popped one in her mouth. "Yum!"

"Glad you like it." Cody chuckled then faced Pappy. "Care to show me where I can find your tools?"

Pappy pushed up from the table. "Might as well. Ain't got nothing better to do, and these hens need their space to keep clucking."

Heat collided against Katherine's cheeks, and she avoided Cody's curiosity as he followed her grandfather into the garage.

Sighing, she dropped into a chair in front of Nora. Not only was Cody handsome and kind, he handled her grandfather like a pro and was great with kids. Not to mention being good with his hands if he could maintain the clunker she'd be driving around.

Marie settled in the seat beside her. "I'm sorry about the accident. Are you okay?"

She nodded. "Yeah, but I don't want to think about what could have happened. I've never been so scared."

"Then we won't talk about it," Marie said. "Instead, we can discuss the cutie patootie deputy who's braving your grandfather so he can change your oil. He seems like a really nice guy. Could there be something between you two?"

A punch of guilt accompanied the excitement over the idea of exploring the possibilities with Cody. "It's too soon."

Reaching across the table, Marie took hold of Katherine's hand. "There's no time limit on when it's right for you to find happiness with someone else. Follow your gut and know that Theo wouldn't want you to spend the rest of your life alone. He loved you so much. He'd want you to be happy. Whether that's with the hottie in the garage or someone else, it doesn't matter. Just know finding love again doesn't replace Theo. It's a testament to the wonderful marriage you shared."

Emotions choked her windpipe. "What do you mean?"

"If you hadn't experienced so much joy and love with Theo, there'd be no reason to try and find it again. Theo showed you what true love is. Maybe it's time to see if you have a second act waiting."

A chunk of the guilt clinging to her heart fell away. Marie was right. Her marriage had been the stuff every little girl dreams about. She'd thought that meant she'd had her chance, no more shots left for her. But maybe she'd been looking at it the wrong way. Because Theo had showered her with so much love, she knew what she deserved—what she wanted in a future partner.

And maybe wanting Cody wasn't such a bad thing after all.

A WALL of stale air greeted Cody the second he stepped foot in the dingy garage. The sun struggled to peek through the dirt smeared on the windows. A truck almost as old as Katherine's grandpa sat in the middle of the room. A long workbench took up one wall, shelves lined with all kinds of crap took up another.

Lewis pushed the white button to lift the garage door then ambled over to the shelves. "You work with cars a lot?"

"No, sir." He stayed a step behind the old man. He didn't want to crowd him but stayed close in case the guy fell over. Hell, he appeared so frail Cody was afraid the slight breeze blowing in would knock him right off his feet.

"What makes you think you can change the oil?" Lewis rummaged through boxes until he found one filled with bottles of motor oil.

Cody hurried to take it from him then carried the box to the workbench. "I change my own oil. Used to do my old man's, and his truck was a lot like this one. The way I grew up, if you wanted something fixed you either fixed it yourself or wasted time staring at a broken piece of junk."

Lewis snorted out a laugh. "I respect that. Grew up much the same way and tried my damndest to instill that in my grandkids. Their mother understood hard work. Their father, well, I won't go into what I think of that guy."

Curiosity threatened to raise his brow, but instinct told Cody to keep a neutral expression. He liked Mike Wells a hell of a lot and didn't want to be caught by Katherine or anyone else speaking ill of his former boss. "Your grandchildren seem pretty capable of taking care of themselves."

Lewis gave one decisive nod. "Sure are. Especially Katherine. She's the toughest of the bunch if you ask me, but don't tell her I said that."

"Your secret's safe with me," Cody said.

While Lewis shuffled around searching for the tools needed to do the job, Cody unbuttoned his unform shirt at the wrists and rolled up his shirtsleeves. He popped the hood of the truck and located the oil fill trap and plug. "I'm gonna need to drain this. You got a tray I can use for the old oil?"

"Said I got everything you needed, didn't I?" Lewis found a

tray and handed it over. "I lined everything else you might need on the workbench."

"Appreciate it."

He went to work draining the oil, all the while feeling the heat of Lewis's gray eyes on him. When it was time to swap out the filter, he wiped his stained hands on his pantlegs and turned toward the wooden bench.

"Filter's on the left of the wrench," Lewis said. He sat on a backless stool with his spine straight and arms across his chest. A weary look of appreciation on his wrinkled face.

"Thanks." He found the right box and lifted the flap of the cardboard.

"Be careful with her," Lewis said.

Frowning, Cody stilled with the filter halfway out of the box. "The truck? I promise I know what I'm doing."

Closing his eyes, Lewis clicked his tongue and shook his head. When he opened his eyes again, a mixture of worry and pain shone through. "That's not who I'm talking about."

A lump wedged in Cody's throat and every word in the English language left his brain.

"Like I said," Lewis continued. "She's tough. But that doesn't mean she should have to be. The rug's been yanked out from under that girl's feet more than once. First when her mom died, then with what happened to Theo. I'd hate to see it happen a third time. And if there's even one shred of you that thinks you might cause her pain, walk away now."

"Sir, I'm just doing my job. Helping her out because she's had some bad things happen the last couple days."

Another snort came from Lewis, but this one didn't hold an ounce of amusement. "We both know you're doing more than what the sheriff expects of you, especially since the sheriff just happens to be her brother."

The musty air thickened around him, and Cody coughed to clear his throat. Two days ago, Katherine was nothing more than another woman in town who didn't give him a second glance. Had he always found her attractive? Sure. But he'd never imagined there could be anything between them.

That had changed in less than forty-eight hours, at least on his side, and her grandfather had no qualms about calling him out. Something he respected even if it made him nervous as hell.

"Katherine and I are friends, new ones at that. She's a nice woman and I want to make sure she's safe. My intentions are good, that I can promise, but I'm not sure what else there is to say. I know about what happened to Katherine's husband, and I'd never do anything to disrespect what she shared with Theo or make her uncomfortable. No matter what the future holds, it's up to Katherine to give me the green light on anything that could possibly exist there."

Lewis worked his jaw back and forth as if chewing over his answer.

Sweat dotted Cody's hairline and his nerves bunched up, as though this man's opinion was the final verdict in something that may not even be a possibility.

"Well, all right then. How about we finish changing this oil?"

Relieved, Cody let out a long breath. If he did want some kind of a future with Katherine, there were a lot of obstacles to overcome. At least he'd just bypassed one of them.

With his focus back on task, he removed the filter from the box just as the kitchen door banged open.

Katherine stood on the step with her phone in her hand. Her gaze stayed glued to the screen before she glanced up and met his eye. "My security system is going off. Somebody's at my house."

8

Katherine's heart pounded faster than the spinning tires of Cody's cruiser speeding toward town. She ran her hands up and down the coarse denim that covered her thighs, gaze fixed out the window.

A soft touch on her hand jerked her attention over to Cody.

He rested his palm over the back of her hand and flicked her a quick glance before returning his focus in front of him. "No matter what we find, at least we know that nobody was injured. The house was empty. But if you don't stop, you're going to rub a hole in your jeans."

Clinging to that thought, she squeezed his hand. Grateful didn't even come close to describing the depth of her emotions for Cody and the gentle calm he carried with him.

"You're right. As freaked out as I am that this guy knows where I live, I can at least be thankful he found an empty house." Her phone rang, interrupting her thoughts, and she hurried to answer when she spied her brother's name on the screen. She activated speaker phone so Cody could hear the conversation. "Hey, Owen. You at my place?"

"Dad and I just got here. A window's busted but that

appears to be the extent of the damage. Once you arrive we'll look at the footage. See if we can get any distinguishing features of the vandal. You close?"

"We're about a minute away."

"We?"

"Me and Cody." Saying his name reminded her that she still held his hand. She should release it, but dammit, she didn't want to.

"I thought you were getting Pappy's truck," Owen said.

"Pappy insisted it needed an oil change. Cody was in the middle of changing it when the alarm went off on my phone."

Cody turned onto her street.

The sight of blue and red lights slashing through the sky turned her stomach. "We're about to pull up the drive. I'll talk to you in a second."

"He didn't sound thrilled to hear you were still with me," Cody said.

"He's just stressed and scared. He takes his duties as older brother seriously and this has him terrified for my safety. Leave it to Owen to think something bad happening to me makes him a failure."

"He's the sheriff. It's his job to catch the bad guy. The fact that he hasn't yet, and you're the one paying the price, has to weigh heavy." Cody maneuvered his cruiser behind Owen's and shifted into park while keeping her hand tucked in his. "You ready?"

"Not really. This house has always been a safe space. A home. It's never been the same since Theo died, and now it's tainted. I don't know if I can face it."

"Then don't."

She blinked at the casualness of his suggestion. "What do you mean?"

"Give your brother the code to your security system. He

doesn't need you here to look at it. Let him and everyone else do their jobs."

"And what do I do?"

He lifted a shoulder. "What do you want to do?"

She sighed and spied her dad heading her way. "Disappear."

"All right. Then let's go."

She faced him with wide eyes. Her heart sped up, pulsing against the inside of her wrists. "What?"

"If you'd feel safer leaving town for a while, we'll leave. We'll grab some things, get Ollie, and find somewhere to lay low until this blows over."

The side of her mouth inched up. As good as it sounded to leave town with Cody and Ollie, it wouldn't be right. "My family would love that."

He wrinkled his nose. "I don't care what your family thinks. All I care about is making sure you feel comfortable and protected. I'm here for whatever you need." He squeezed her hand before slipping his palm away from hers then stepping out of the car. Before he shut the door, he leaned his forearm on the top of the vehicle. "I got you. Remember that."

A knot formed at the base of her throat, stealing her words. She nodded and hurried out the passenger side of the door before his sincerity brought tears to her eyes.

Her dad marched over the concrete drive, a deep frown pulling down the sides of his face. "I hate that I keep seeing you like this. Something's got to give."

"Where's Owen?" She understood her father's stance and agreed. Standing in her driveway rehashing everything wouldn't help. She just wanted to know the extent of the damage to her home and figure out the next best move.

Mike hooked a thumb over his shoulder. "Inside."

"How bad is it?"

"Broken window. Something was thrown inside." Mike

rubbed the back of his neck and averted his eyes, casting his gaze to his feet.

She swallowed the bile rising up her throat.

"I can head in and check out the footage with him if you want," Cody said.

As much as she liked the idea of not having to watch her house being vandalized, she needed to see the destruction for herself. "We'll all watch."

He nodded then waited for her to make her way up the sidewalk to the front porch. Glass glimmered in the sunlight, the window looking into the living room smashed. The bile hit the back of her palate. She struggled to keep it from spewing out of her mouth and onto the daisies on the other side of the railing.

Cody rested a hand on the small of her back. "You're okay."

She relaxed against his touch. His statement was exactly what she needed. Not a question of whether or not she could handle what came next, but a firm declaration that she could handle whatever was inside the house.

Her father darted his gaze between the two of them, the deep V between his eyebrows comically low. But he kept his opinions to himself as he led the way inside.

Owen stood with Tommy in the living room. Both men had their arms crossed over their chest, staring at something laying on the floor.

"She's here," Mike said.

Both men glanced up, each aiming a confused frown toward Cody.

Cody's hand didn't budge. It remained a steady rock on her back, gently encouraging her to keep moving.

"What are you both looking at?" she asked.

Tommy coughed and gestured toward the floor.

Owen scowled with his narrowed gaze fixed on Cody.

"Might as well tell her what we found inside the living room before looking at the footage." Mike stood in the center of the small group.

Appreciation washed over her. If she didn't understand her feelings for Cody right now, the last thing she wanted was her brothers interfering or needing to speak on why she wanted Cody right now.

The thought smashed against her like whatever the hell had burst through her window. The last thing she expected was a bone-deep *need* for anyone besides her son at this point in her life. How had her world shifted upside down so quickly?

Owen shoved a hand through his hair then pointed in the same direction Tommy had indicated. "Someone threw a clock through your window."

"Excuse me?" If she'd had a million guesses for what she'd find, she'd never have guessed that.

"With a note. We'll bag it and take it into evidence, but the message he left is loud and clear."

Tearing herself away from Cody, she took two steps forward and crouched to get a better look at the red clock. The hands ticked away, even if she couldn't see them behind the words that made her blood turn to ice.

Time's up.

CODY STARED down at the clock. The threat stared back at him, and he clenched his jaw so tight he feared his molars might crack.

Katherine straightened and swayed on her feet.

He was next to her in a heartbeat. He wrapped on arm around the small of her back and cupped his other palm around her elbow. "Let's sit down. How about the kitchen?"

She nodded and let him guide her down the hall to the large eat-in kitchen.

The heat of three sets of eyes singed the back of his neck, but he didn't care as he pulled out a chair and helped Katherine sit. He was serious earlier. He liked her family, and if anything was ever destined to happen between them, he wanted them to accept him, but their opinions were not his priority.

Katherine and her safety were.

"I...I don't understand. Time's up? What the hell does that mean?" She threw her hands in the air before dropping her head to rest in her palms. "I mean, I know what it *means*, but why? I've racked my brain, searching for anyone I could have wronged or upset. Nobody comes to mind. How could I have pissed off someone so bad they'd try to kill me? And now they've come to my private space, the home where my son rests his head, and threatened me."

Owen, Tommy, and Mike stood around the table, flanking her from all sides like a human shield.

"What about a pissed off patient?" Mike asked. "We had a case not too long ago where a disgruntled family member came back and took his anger out on a doctor."

Cody recalled the case Mike spoke about. Dr. Jenna Simon had been caught in the middle of a widower who needed to blame his wife's death on someone, and she'd been the unlucky target. It wasn't far-fetched to believe something similar could happen again.

Katherine shook her head. "Nothing that comes to mind, but I can call my boss and have him pull up recent records."

"You should do that now," Owen said. "And while you're on the phone, see if you can take some time off work. This guy knows your routine. Where you work and live. You can't just go back to your job like nothing's happened. I'm sure your boss will understand."

She let out a long breath. "I don't have much personal time. I took off a lot after Theo died."

"It's not like you're asking to take a vacation for the hell of it," Cody said, hating she found herself in this position. "The only other option is to have someone with you the entire time you work. Something tells me that wouldn't fly at a hospital."

That coaxed a bit of a smile from her. "Probably not."

"Then it's settled," Mike said. "You take a few days off. You and Ollie will stay with me."

A tiny bit of tension stiffened Katherine's neck. She kept her head down, eyes on the table.

His blood pressure spiked. The idea of her being away from him, entrusted to a good man like her father, made his nerves go haywire. Not to mention he could read her like a damn book. She didn't like the idea of staying with her dad. She'd told him earlier she had to temper her own emotions to make sure her family was okay. She shouldn't have to worry about anyone else right now.

Katherine finally glanced up and aimed a tight smile at her dad. "Are you sure that's a good idea?"

"Why wouldn't it be?" Mike asked.

"Because if this guy has followed Katherine long enough to know her patterns, he's probably aware of where her family lives," Cody said.

If looks could kill, the expression on Mike's face would have sent Cody to the morgue. "And if he does, then we'll handle him. Hell, I'll have Tommy and Owen stay and we'll all keep guard twenty-four damn hours a day until this bastard is found."

Katherine sighed. "You can't do that. The sheriff's department is small enough as it is. The sheriff and one deputy can't both protect me. There will be no one around to catch the guy who wants me dead."

Owen winced. "I'm the sheriff. I can decide what the department can handle. Besides, Cody wants to make himself useful. He can head up the investigation while we keep you safe."

He might appreciate his boss' confidence in him, but deep down he understood it had more to do with keeping him away from Katherine than wanting him to be the one who made the arrest.

A familiar feeling of being shoved aside, looked down on for reasons beyond his control, fisted his hands at his side. He wasn't a kid anymore. Wasn't afraid to stand up for himself and go after what he wanted—what he deserved.

"She should stay with me," he said.

Mike's stare hardened to stone. "Excuse me?"

Cody struggled not to squirm, but standing in front of Katherine's overprotective family while claiming she should stay with him was tougher than staring down an armed robber. "I live out of town and no way this guy knows where my house is. Why would he? I've never spent time with Katherine. She's never been to my home. I can stick close to her and Ollie, keeping them both safe, while the rest of the department nails this guy's ass to the wall."

Tommy snorted. "You think my sister would just take her kid and stay with you?"

"Maybe you should direct that question at me," Katherine snapped, raising to her feet. "Because, honestly, that sounds like a better idea then you all standing over me every day until this is over."

Owen scuffed. "Seriously? What will you tell Ollie?"

"As much as we have to in order to let him know he needs to be careful, but not too much to scare him." The words were out of Cody's mouth before he could stop them. Hell, Ollie wasn't his kid. He had no right to say what Katherine should or shouldn't tell her child. But he'd spent a lifetime battling against lies and manipulation, and if he had any influence over how this played out, he opted to be as honest as possible.

And the curve of Katherine's lips told him he'd said the right thing.

"I don't know," Mike said. "I'd feel better with you and Ollie under my roof."

"And I'd feel better knowing you're out there with Owen and Tommy helping to make this nightmare stop. This feels right. Trust me," Katherine said.

"It's not you I'm worried about." Mike kept his focus directly fixed on Cody.

He stood his ground. This was Katherine's call. He'd support whatever she decided.

Katherine huffed out an irritated breath. "Enough bullshit, Dad. I know you mean well, but Cody has been by my side from the moment this started. I don't just trust him with my life, but with Ollie's."

Her words tightened his chest and caused his eyes to burn. Dammit, he needed to get a grip before he made an ass of himself and cried.

But even if tears slid from his eyes, he didn't give a shit. All that mattered was the trust Katherine placed in him, and nothing short of a bullet in his chest would stop him from keeping her and her son alive.

9

Twisting the fidget spinner between her fingers, Katherine searched for Ollie at the shelter. Cody agreed to wait on the porch. Not only did she want an opportunity to discuss the situation with her son before she introduced him to Cody, but she also didn't want his presence to alarm Beth or any other woman who could show up in distress.

The sound of giggling drew her into the library on the main floor. She always loved this room. The dark green walls were like a comforting hug, and the row of books lining the built-in shelves made her wish she had hours to pour over the pages. And when a fire was lit, it took all her effort not to pour herself a glass of wine and curl onto the oversized sofa.

The boys weren't interested in the books or the fireplace. Instead, Ollie and Jimmy sat in the corner looking through trading cards from one of the cartoons they both loved.

"Hey, you two," she said, the sing-song quality of her voice ringing false. "Sorry I took so long, but something came up. Here's the fidget spinner you wanted to see."

The boys jumped to their feet and ran across the room, their cards forgotten on the floor behind them.

Ollie threw his arms around her waist before grabbing the toy from her outstretched hand. "Thanks, Mom!"

"Yeah, Ms. Katherine," Jimmy said. "You're the best!"

She spent a minute watching the boys light up and play with the toy before interrupting their fun. "Jimmy, can you find Elsie for a second? I need to speak with Ollie."

"You can show her my toy." Ollie handed over the spinner.

"She'll love it." Jimmy took the toy and ran from the room.

"That was nice of you," she said, pride swelling her chest at his generosity. He'd always been such a sweet kid. She was glad to see that the blows of life hadn't changed him. "Come sit with me." Taking his hand, she led him to the sofa.

He hopped up and settled in close to her.

She'd spoken with Cody on the way to the shelter about the best way to approach Ollie. But now that the moment was here, dread slowed her thoughts. She didn't want to spook him but also didn't want to lie.

"The reason it took me so long to get back with your toy is because there was an issue."

He frowned, fear inching into his big brown eyes. "What happened?"

"Someone is mad at Mommy. Grandpa, Uncle Owen, and Uncle Tommy are looking for him so they can make sure he can't hurt me. But until then, we can't stay at our house." She took a moment to gauge his reaction. When he seemed okay, she continued. "We're going to spend a few days with a friend. Like a little vacation."

He perked up. "With Jimmy and Elsie?"

She smiled down at him. "No, honey. A friend who works with Uncle Owen and Uncle Tommy."

Frowning, he clutched his little hands in his lap. "Do I know him?"

"He was friends with your daddy." Okay, so that might be a bit of an exaggeration, but her gut told her that would put Ollie a little more at ease.

"Does he have a pool?"

The seriousness of the question lifted her lips. "I don't think so. Why do you ask?"

"You said it's like vacation," he said, shrugging. "We *always* swim when we go on vacation."

Chuckling, she squeezed him in a side hug. "That's true. Swimming might not be an option, especially since it's really not that warm, but he does have a dog."

Excitement vibrated through him, and he shot to his feet. "Really? A big one or a little one? What's its name? Can we play fetch?"

She held up her hands. "I don't have any answers for you, silly. But if you're ready to meet my friend, we can head outside and you can ask him all the questions you want."

He nibbled on his thumbnail. "Is your friend nice?"

"He's very nice."

"Okay, let's go." He sprinted toward the door.

"Wait for me." She hurried after him, not wanting him out of her sight in case something—or someone—waited outside. "We need to tell Elsie and Jimmy goodbye."

Ollie switched directions and headed toward the store at the back of the shelter.

Katherine reached him at the doorway and circled her arms around his neck to pull him close. He must have sensed her need to be near him because he didn't struggle against her hug like he'd started to do lately. She gave Elsie a quick, watered down version of what was happening and promised to call her later before steering Ollie back toward the front door.

"Wait!" Jimmy yelled and ran out to the hallway. "Here's your fidget spinner. It's super cool."

Ollie grinned. "Thanks." He took back his toy and gave a little wave before stepping outside.

The warm spring sun hit Katherine in the face. She drew in a deep breath, filling her lungs with crisp, mountain air. She kept one hand on Ollie's slim shoulder and walked beside him down the porch steps to the driveway.

Cody stood on the sidewalk. He lifted his hand in greeting.

She wiggled her fingers in a come-here motion. Nerves bunched in her core, vibrating her insides. She wanted Ollie to like Cody. Wanted the two of them to like each other. She wasn't exactly sure what that meant but understood that how these two got along would impact the way she navigated any attachment to Cody.

Because even if she might be ready to take a step toward her new future, it didn't mean Ollie was. And Ollie would always be her number one priority.

Reading her signal, Cody shoved his hands in the pockets of his trousers. With his shirtsleeves pushed up to his elbows, his muscular forearms stood out against his khaki uniform.

Saliva pooled in her mouth, and she cleared her throat to clear any lingering desire from her system. Dang, how was it possible for these feelings to sneak up so suddenly for someone she'd known her entire life?

"Hi, Ollie. I'm Cody. It's so nice to meet you." He slid one hand out from his pocket and extended it toward Ollie.

Ollie scrunched his nose. "Why's your hand dirty?"

Cody twisted his wrist to look at his palm and shrugged. "I was changing the oil on your Pappy's truck. I must have gotten some on me and haven't had a chance to wash it off."

"Wow," Ollie said, eyes widening. "You like cars? Do you like Hot Wheels?"

"I like all kinds of stuff." Cody grinned and kept his attention squarely on Ollie.

Katherine's toes curled in her sneakers. She couldn't help but wonder if she was one of those things he could like.

"And you have a dog?"

"Yep. Her name is Bailey. She's going to love you."

Ollie finally fit his little hand in Cody's and gave one big shake. "Can't wait to meet her. She can play cars with us. Mom, did you pack my toys? I want to play with Cody and Bailey."

He scampered ahead and climbed into the back of Cody's cruiser.

Cody's gaze latched onto hers and the side of his mouth slid up.

A shiver raced down her spine. Her son wasn't the only one who wanted to play with Cody, but she'd keep that thought to herself. At least for a little while longer.

CODY HOPED Katherine and Ollie couldn't see the anxiousness creeping over him as he led them up his porch and fished his keys out of his pocket. So far, Ollie seemed to like him. At least the boy's constant chatter on the drive to his house smothered any tension he or Katherine experienced.

A big, loud bark boomed from inside.

"Be prepared. Bailey's a sweet girl, but she doesn't understand how big she is. She can get a little excited. Make sure she knows you're the boss, okay?"

Ollie puffed up his chest. "I'm the boss," he repeated.

"I'll introduce you both to her then come out to grab your bags."

"I can help with that," Katherine said. "No need to fuss over us."

He wanted to argue, to admit he wanted nothing more than to fuss over them. Give them whatever they needed to make their lives a little more comfortable. But he didn't want her to feel smothered or as if he was swooping in and taking control.

Frantic barking told him he better open the door before Bailey burst through the front window. He unlocked the door and swung it open, stepping over the threshold to stop his dog from barging outside and knocking poor Ollie on his backside.

"Hey, girl. Calm down. I brought some new friends for you, but you have to sit." He crouched and looped an arm over the dog's neck to pin her in place.

Excitement vibrated Bailey's entire body, her tail thumping against the wooden planks of the porch.

Katherine covered her mouth with her hands. "Oh my gosh, she's so cute!"

"Can I pet her?" Ollie asked, taking one step forward.

"Go for it," Cody said. "But remember. You're in charge."

Ollie lifted a hand for the dog to smell, and when Bailey's giant tongue shot out to lick him, he giggled. He erased the distance between them and threw his arms around the dog.

Bailey sat still, her mouth open in a dopey smile.

Katherine patted the top of Bailey's head. "She's so fluffy. And big. I swear she looks more like a curly-haired wolf than a dog. How long have you had her?"

"A couple of years." He didn't want to go into how Bailey had ended up in his care. Especially in front of Ollie. "Let's head inside."

Bailey bounded in the house as if wanting to lead the tour. She ran in a giant circle in the living room and jumped in the air like a kid on a damn trampoline.

Ollie's laughter made the dog's antics welcome for once. "She's funny. Does she fetch?"

Cody flicked a wrist toward a basket in the corner of the room. "All her toys are in there. She'll take any kind of attention you can give her." He glanced at Katherine and her wide smile as she watched her son play with the dog turned him into a puddle of mush. "I'll grab the bags now while he's having fun. You can help if you want or stay and join in the excitement."

"If you don't mind, I think I'll stay. Keep an eye on him just in case."

Although he knew without a shadow of a doubt Bailey wouldn't do anything on purpose to hurt the boy, he understood her wanting to keep an eye on her son with a new to her dog.

"I'll be right back."

He hurried outside to secure their bags and brought them back inside.

"Do you want to see your room?" he asked Ollie. "I'm sure Bailey will follow you. Heck, she'll probably want to sleep with you tonight if your mom's okay with it, but just know she's a bed hog."

"She's like a giant pillow," Ollie said. "Can she sleep with me, Mom? Please!"

"Unless you're planning on going to bed before dinner, we can discuss this later. Here, let me help you with those." She grabbed her duffle from Cody, her fingers brushing against his.

He gritted his teeth at his body's reaction to her simple touch. No way he'd survive having her stay in his home if he couldn't keep a tighter leash on his emotions.

Needing some space, he led the way down the hall. "I have two rooms. Ollie, you can sleep in this one." He flipped on the light to the guest room and set the child's bag on the floor, leaning the superhero suitcase against the wall. "Looks like your mom packed you enough stuff to stay for a month."

"That'd be so much fun." Ollie ran past him and jumped onto the bed. He laid on his back and settled his hands behind his head as he stared up at the ceiling. "Can we stay that long, Mom?"

Katherine's smile tightened. "I'm not sure how long we'll be here, buddy. Let's just enjoy the time we have."

Bailey barked as if in agreement and leapt into the bed, curling against Ollie and using his belly as a pillow.

"Well, they look comfortable enough," he said, loving the way the little boy fit right in. "I'll take you across the hall to where you'll be staying."

She frowned and turned her head away from Ollie so he couldn't hear their conversation. "I thought you said you have two bedrooms," she whispered.

"I do."

"You want me to sleep with you in your room?" Her mouth fell open and her cheeks turned bright red.

A hundred images flashed in his mind, probably making his face as red as hers, and he cleared his throat. "Yes, I want you to sleep in my room but no, not with me."

"Wait, I don't understand. Where do you plan to sleep then?"

"The couch pulls out to a bed. I'll sleep in the living room."

"No way," she said, shaking her head. "I can stay in here with Ollie. We've put you out enough already. There's no need for me to steal your room, too."

"You aren't stealing anything, and you're not putting me out. I want you here, and I want you in my bed."

Desire flashed in her eyes and her tongue darted out to lick her bottom lip.

His stomach muscles clenched and a part of his anatomy he couldn't control strained against his pants. Shit. Even if what he said was true in every possible way, he had to figure out how to get his giant foot out of his mouth.

Swallowing hard, he averted her gaze and squeezed the back of his neck. "What I meant to say is you've had a hard couple of days. You need a comfortable place to rest. One without a little boy and probably a dog keeping you awake. Besides, being in the living room keeps me more alert, and I want to make sure I hear anything just in case."

A small smile played on her lips. "Well, if you're sure, the space would be nice. But if the sofa is too uncomfortable, just say the word and I'll join Ollie and give you back your room."

Decision made, he carried her things across the hall and set them down. "Make yourself at home. I need to make a call."

Before she could respond, he hurried to the back deck and inhaled a deep breath. Nope. He definitely wouldn't survive Katherine in his home. He was nothing more than a dead man walking.

10

K atherine kept her ears tuned into Ollie's giggles as he continued to play with Bailey across the hall. The knot of tension tying up her insides loosened. Chaos might have disrupted her world, but her son was clearly happy. She could only hope that continued for however long they stayed with Cody.

Cody.

Just thinking about him was enough to make tingles of excitement burst in the pit of her stomach. She pressed her hands to her tummy and sighed. She'd loved Theo with her entire being, but it'd been a long time since she felt the first pangs of...what? Desire? Romance? Love?

Snorting out a laugh, she grabbed her bag and set it on the bench in front of the king-sized bed. Love was something that was earned, something that grew over time. After months and months of learning about and spending time with someone. Her life wasn't some silly movie where the clouds parted and trumpets played, cluing everyone into the leading hero in her story.

No, she'd had true love—had a hero. Marie was right. That

didn't mean she couldn't have it again, but she wasn't a teenager who believed in love at first sight anymore. She was a grown woman with responsibilities and a son. She had to take her time. Move slowly. Understand her own heart before she opened it up to anyone else.

Logic in place, she set her folded clothes out on the bed and placed her toiletries in the en suite bathroom. Cody had said to make herself comfortable. She hoped she wasn't pushing it too far, but she really didn't want to live out of a suitcase.

Returning to the bedroom, she fisted her hands on her hips and studied the space. A navy blue comforter fit neatly over the mattress. Dark wood made up a long dresser pressed against one wall, a flatscreen television mounted above it. Four windows connected at an angle and created a cozy sitting nook where two chairs sat with a stand between. With the shades open, she could spy the mountains practically in the back yard.

Everything was tidy, neatly put in place, and without a speck of dust.

A framed photo of a little boy and who she assumed was his mother stood on the nightstand. Sitting on the bed, she picked it up and ran her finger over the face of the child.

A light tap at the door caught her attention. She glanced up to find Cody leaning against the doorjamb, his arms crossed over his chest and intrigue lifting his brow. "What cha doing?"

She flipped the photo around for him to see. "Is this you?"

"Yeah, me and my mom."

"She's beautiful. Are you two still close?"

Frowning, he took a step forward and tilted his head to the side. "She died when I was in middle school."

Guilt and shame smacked Katherine upside the head. "I'm so sorry. How did I not know that?"

"There's a lot about me you never knew."

She patted the bed beside her, waiting for him to sit before speaking again. "I was an idiot. A silly girl caught in her own world. I'm sorry about your mother. I understand how hard it is to lose your mom. Especially so young."

"Hmm," he said, the sound noncommittal.

"What is it?"

"No, you're right. A part of what we experienced is very similar."

"And the other part?"

He turned to face her, his lips swished to the side as if uncertain he could confide in her.

Wanting to be there for him in the same way he'd been there for her, she rested her hand on his hard thigh. "Tell me. Please."

"When my mom died, I was left with a shitty father and asshole of a brother. I had no one to comfort me. No one to care for me. I was all alone. I'm glad that part of our story differs."

More shame burrowed into her gut. "I can't imagine how hard that must have been. Losing your mother was difficult enough. My family can be a pain in the ass sometimes, but they're always there. Always supporting me in every way possible. Even if they're over protectiveness can be a little much sometimes. I hate that they aimed it at you earlier."

He shrugged and a rested a hand on top of hers. "It's great you have them, and them looking after you doesn't bother me. They should be on guard as far as I'm concerned."

The gravelly tone of his voice hitched her breath. "Oh really? Why's that?"

He lifted their joined hands. "Something tells me they're as terrified of this as I am."

She frowned, trying to make sense of his words. "And what do you have to be afraid of?"

"You."

Caught off guard, she blinked twice, trying to decipher his response. "What do you mean?"

"I'm going to be honest with you, because it's the only way I know how to be. Something is building on my end of this thing. It's surprised the hell out of me, and I'm not sure what it means. But I know I could fall hard for you. You hold all the power here. And as much as I hate to admit it, you could destroy me."

She couldn't stop her mouth from dropping open. She'd never had a man hit her with so much truth, been so vulnerable so quick. With Theo, they'd met in grade school and been joined at the hip since before she could remember. Their love had grown from something sweet and innocent into something strong and real. It had never been this out of nowhere, slap you in the face kind of attraction.

Her mind whirling, she tried to erase the smack-gobbed expression off her face. "Trust me, I'm scared too. I never expected to feel anything for anyone after Theo died—never wanted to. I had my chance and loved every minute of it. Why should I be special enough to find that kind of happiness more than once?"

He tucked a strand of hair behind her ear, letting his fingers linger along her jawline. "Everyone in this life deserves to find as much damn happiness as possible. Even someone like me."

The fact he still saw himself as less-than gutted her. "Especially someone like you. You've taken in me and my son, determined to keep us safe. You've been my rock the last couple of days. Heck, you've went head-to-head with not only my dad and brothers but my grandpa."

He grinned. "He told me to leave you alone if I planned to hurt you."

"And what did you say?"

"I'd rather die than hurt you."

His words were like a healing balm on her battered heart, and she knew deep down to her toes he meant it.

Her gaze flicked to his mouth. His parted lips drew her forward like a magnet. She didn't want to wait for him to make a move, didn't want to sit and wonder what it'd be like to kiss him. Before she could talk herself out of it, she pressed her lips to his and an explosion of stars burst behind her closed eyelids.

His palm cradled her jaw, his touch tender, and he moved his mouth slowly over hers.

She moved closer, wanting more.

"Mom! I'm hungry, can I have a snack?"

Her son's little voice from across the hall was like a bucket of icy water over her head. She broke away.

Cody kept his hand smoothed against her face. He brushed the pad of his thumb over her lips. "You're going to be the death of me."

She grinned. "I sure hope not."

He chuckled. "Never thought I'd be asking a beautiful woman this, but can you get out of my bedroom for a second?"

She pulled back, humiliation scorching her veins. "I... I'm sorry."

"I need to change, and I don't think that's something you should stick around for. At least not yet." He winked then kissed her cheek before standing.

Dear Lord. A part of her didn't want to get off the bed— wanted to stick around for a show. Another part had to feed her son who waited in the room across the hall.

Logic won out and she hopped to her feet. "Is it all right if I get Ollie something to eat?"

"Grab whatever you'd like. Once I get changed, I can start dinner. Barbeque chicken sound good?"

"Sounds great."

She walked out of the room, closing the door behind her. Chicken would be great, but she could think of something else that sounded so much better.

∾

THE HEAT of the grill threatened to singe Cody's eyebrows. He wiped his forearm across his brow to mop away his sweat. The barbecue sauce slathered on the chicken sizzled, tempting him to slide his finger through the thick goo to sneak a taste.

Katherine stepped onto the deck, carrying a bowl of salad. She wore a fitted long-sleeved shirt and her long hair hung down her back. A different kind of temptation tightened his gut.

"It's so nice, I figured we could eat outside." She set the bowl in the middle of the patio table. "This view is amazing."

"It sure is," he said, unable to keep his eyes off her.

Her gaze snapped up, meeting his. The prettiest blush touched her cheeks.

The memory of their earlier kiss hit him with the force of a landslide, and he took a step toward her. One taste wasn't enough. It only fueled the fire building inside him.

"Bailey wants to play fetch." Ollie's excited yell announced the dynamic duo seconds before the boy and dog sprinted across the deck and down the stairs to the backyard.

Clearing his throat, he returned to his task and flipped the chicken. "Almost done here. I'll head in to grab plates."

"I can do that," Katherine said.

"No, it's fine. Sit and relax."

He might have to make a couple trips, but he needed some space from Katherine, not seeing her at home in his kitchen.

"Are you sure? I like my hands to stay busy. Keeps my mind off...other things."

The way her voice dipped, he wasn't sure if she meant she wanted her mind off the reason she was here or off of him.

"You can make sure the chicken doesn't burn." He handed over the tongs.

Something flashed in her eyes as she took the utensil and stared at the grill.

"Katherine?"

"Hmm?" she asked, blinking away whatever emotion had paralyzed her.

"Are you all right?"

She sighed then forced a small smile. "I'm fine. Just not used to manning the grill. That was always Theo's job. He guarded it like he'd been anointed by God himself as chief barbecuer. Sorry."

"Don't ever apologize for talking about Theo. He's a part of your story, of Ollie's story, forever. He deserves to be remembered."

Tears clouded her eyes, and she reached a hand out for him.

He wasted no time in slipping his palm in hers then closing his fingers around her slender hand.

"Thank you. For everything," she whispered.

He brought her hand to his lips and pressed a quick kiss to her knuckles. "I told you. I've got you. And I don't mean just keeping you safe until whoever is after you is caught."

Breaking his hold, he left her slack jawed and hurried into the kitchen.

He let out a long, shuddering breath as he found plates in the cabinet and grabbed silverware from the drawer. Hesitating beside the wine rack, he considered grabbing a bottle of white but left it untouched. He needed a clear head, and he didn't know if she even drank alcohol.

Hell, there was a lot he didn't know about her. The thought excited him, made him want to spend time discovering all he could about her. But he couldn't appear too eager. Had to match her pace as they figured out their shit.

He carried everything outside and placed it on the table. "What about a drink?"

"Any chance you have a beer?" She wrinkled her nose in the cutest way.

"Beer, huh? I pegged you as a white wine kind of woman."

She narrowed her gaze, lips curved just enough for her dimples to appear. "I'm not sure if I should take that as a compliment or not."

"Take it any way you want, but I'll grab the drinks while you decide if you're offended."

She threw her head back and laughed, the sound combining with Ollie's giggles as he tossed the ball across the yard for a very happy Bailey.

Returning to the kitchen, he found the refillable water bottle Ollie'd used earlier and filled it with ice water then snatched two bottles of his favorite American ale from the fridge. As he stepped outside, Katherine placed the cooked chicken on each of their plates, humming a sweet melody he couldn't quite place. Task complete, she faced the yard. "Ollie, time for dinner. Wash your hands please."

Ollie ran after Bailey. "But Mom. Bailey and I are playing. I can't eat now."

Cody didn't want to step into the middle of their argument but knew exactly how he could help. He set the drinks on the table.

"Give me a second," he said. Popping back inside, he left the door wide open and filled Bailey's food dish with her dinner.

"Hey! Where are you going?" Ollie's voice carried inside seconds before Bailey sprinted into the kitchen.

"Good girl," Cody said then stuck his head out the door. "Dinner time for her, too buddy. Might as well wash up and eat while she's busy. Plenty of time for you two to play when you're both finished."

"Okay!" Ollie sprinted up the stairs and ran past him to the bathroom.

Katherine stood with her fists anchored on her hips. Grinning, she shook her head. "You've got all kinds of tricks, don't you?"

"You don't even know the half of them." He cracked open

one bottle then handed it to her before doing the same to his. He hoisted it in the air and waited for her to tap the neck against his. "To happiness, no matter how we find it, no matter where it takes us."

"To happiness," she repeated, then took a sip of her beer.

He took a long pull of his own, the bitter liquid cool and refreshing as it slid down his throat. Joy like he'd never known settled into his bones as he took in the view. The Smoky Mountains a majestic backdrop for the beautiful woman at his table.

Ollie ran back outside and hopped in his chair. "Looks yummy. Thanks, Cody."

"You're welcome, bud. Dig in."

He held onto the joy, but just underneath it was a new kind of fear. One that told him he could get used to dinners like this —the three of them together, enjoying each other's company. And if anything happened to take it away, it would break his heart.

11

K atherine tip-toed out of the guest bedroom and heaved a large sigh when the giant dog didn't bark and wake Ollie. After a day of running and playing in the fresh air, he'd gone down fast and hard. A miracle in her book. She just hoped he'd stay asleep for the entire night.

Cody glanced up from where he sat on the couch. His laptop rested on his lap. "He asleep?"

"Out like a light. What are you doing?" She nodded toward the computer. "Catching up on work?"

"Looking at some notes your brother sent over."

Intrigue pulled her to his side. "Is it okay if I look, or is that overstepping?"

"Not overstepping at all." He slid over on the couch, making sure there was more than enough space for her.

She settled beside him and tucked her feet beneath her. She stared at the bright screen. "Anything new I should know about?"

He rubbed a hand over the scruff of his jaw. "Not really. Since your attacker showed so much distaste for law enforcement, Owen pulled a few cases where the family of the criminal arrested wasn't happy with the outcome. Nothing stands out, but they made some calls and got nowhere. He asked the local police department to do the same. Someone might be targeting you even if the crime wasn't handled by the sheriff's department."

"Lucky me," she said with a small snort. "None of this makes sense, though." She flicked her wrist toward the screen.

"What do you mean?" He closed the lid and set the computer on the stand beside the sofa.

"Why go after me? Sure, I've got a lot of connections to law enforcement, but I've never worked for my dad. Never been the one who's made an arrest or even the decision to go after anyone." Anger rose as she spoke. She'd had enough shit tossed at her feet. One more thing was enough to push her over the edge.

Cody rested a hand on her knee, grazing his thumb over the soft fabric of her yoga pants. "I get it, and I'm sorry you've been put in this situation. But most of the time logic isn't the criminal's strong suit. That's why we catch them."

Weighing his words, she tilted her head back and forth. "Okay, that makes sense. But it's still bullshit."

"Agreed. When you spoke with your boss, did he offer any insight?"

She recalled the conversation she'd had with Dr. Dempsy before she'd left her home earlier. She hadn't wasted any time letting him know what was going on so he could fill her shifts for the next few days. "He was very supportive, but nothing came to mind for him either. He promised to look into it, though, as well as speak with some co-workers. He said he'd call if they came up with anything."

"And you still haven't thought of anything you were involved with that could piss someone off? Nothing to put a target on your back?"

"Like what?" she asked, raising her hands in the air before

letting them fall again. She dropped one palm onto the top of his knuckles, craving the contact—still befuddled at how natural and easy it was to sit on his couch and hold hands. "I mean, I took Lulu's parking spot by accident at the grocery store and she wasn't very happy, but I stopped by the diner later with cupcakes to smooth things over. I don't think she'd hire a hitman to come after me."

He huffed out a quick laugh and turned his palm over to lace their fingers "Glad to hear it. What about years ago? I'm pulling records of recently released prisoners in the county. I can filter the search by years the prisoners entered the system. Is there a timeframe that stands out where you found yourself in trouble?"

Frustration rippled over her skin, and she pinched the bridge of her nose before letting her head fall back on the sofa. She sunk into the soft cushion, the feel of Cody's hand steady in hers. "Not really. I mean, sure, after my mom died when I was in high school, I had a rebellious couple of months or so but nothing crazy. I drank, went to parties, things typical high school students did but I always steered clear of."

"No run-ins with the law?" A wicked grin played on his lips when he asked.

"God, could you imagine? My dad showing up with a pair of handcuffs and throwing me in a cell? He would have killed me." She chuckled at the thought. "Nah, the few parties I attended left a bad taste in my mouth. I had a friend who was thrilled when I wanted a taste of excitement. She took me to a college party. Some house where her boyfriend lived. I knew right away it wasn't my scene and got the hell out of there."

"Doesn't surprise me," he said, his thumb now grazing the back of her hand instead of her knee.

She pretended to be offended. "Excuse me? What's that supposed to mean?"

"Means you always gave off good girl energy. I can't see you falling in with the wrong crowd. At least not until now."

She grinned. "And you're the wrong crowd?"

He shrugged, amusement leaking from the lines in his face. "Most people in this town always thought so."

Leaning forward, she caught his chin in between her thumb and index finger and forced his eyes to meet hers. "They were wrong, and you've proven that time and time again. Don't let anyone ever make you feel like you aren't an amazing man. And if they do, let me know and I'll kick their ass for you."

His grin matched hers. "Oh yeah? You'd get your hands dirty for me?"

"I'd do just about anything for you."

His smile fell, and he swallowed hard. He closed the gap of space between them and pressed his lips to hers. A simple kiss, sweet and pure. "You've surprised the hell out of me, Katherine Milton."

"Good. I plan to keep doing just that." As much as she wanted to kiss him again, to feel his mouth on hers and see where the night could take them, she held back. Things were moving at lightning speed. Not to mention her son had just fallen asleep in an unfamiliar room down the hall. Chances of him waking and coming to look for her were too high to throw caution to the wind right now.

"The night's still young. Want to watch a movie?" he asked, as if reading her mind.

"What about your work?"

"I'll send it to one of your brothers. I can focus on you and annoy them at the same time." He wiggled his eyebrows, mischief lighting the blue of his eyes.

She laughed and shook her head then winced.

He stiffened beside her. "Are you okay?"

"My neck's a little sore. I've been so consumed with making sure Ollie was comfortable here, I ignored my own discomfort.

Now that he's asleep, it's like my body's decided it's time to feel every last ounce of pain."

"Then it's up to me to take care of you. I'm sorry I didn't think about how what you went through earlier would affect you for a few days. I won't make that mistake again. Sit back, relax, and I'll do whatever I can to make you feel better."

"And how do you plan to do that?"

A sexy half-smile slid up the corner of his mouth. "I told you earlier. I have all kinds of tricks up my sleeve."

Heat licked up her core. She could think of a few ways he could make her feel better, but she'd keep those ideas to herself.

CODY MENTALLY KICKED himself in the ass as he rummaged through his medicine cabinet for over-the-counter medicine for Katherine. Of course she was sore. She'd smashed her SUV into a guardrail earlier.

Grabbing what he needed, he strode out to the kitchen and filled a glass of water and carried everything to Katherine. "This should help with the soreness."

She accepted his offering, swallowing the pills then taking a sip of water. "Thanks, but it's really not too bad. I'm more stiff than anything."

"I have a few ways to help with that, but let's pick a movie first. What are you in the mood to watch?"

"As long as there are no superheroes and it's not a cartoon, I'm down for anything."

He snatched the remote from the end table and opened one of his streaming services until he found a comedy he'd been wanting to watch. "How about this? Something light to make us laugh."

She grinned up at him. "Perfect."

He queued up the movie. "I just need a couple more things."

He popped into the kitchen and grabbed two bags of chips —potato and chocolate—and two bottles of water from the fridge. One beer was enough for him, but he'd ask if she wanted another. He made a pitstop in his office for a bottle of lotion and carried all his findings back to the living room.

Covering her mouth, Katherine smothered a laugh. "What did you find?"

He tossed the snacks onto the empty cushion then set the lotion and water on the coffee table. "I wasn't sure if you'd want something sweet or salty, so I brought both. I know popcorn is more common for movies, but I was afraid the microwave would wake Ollie. I got you water, but if you want something else I can get it, and the lotion is step two in helping with the soreness—as long as you're okay with a little massage." He wiggled his fingers. "But if you aren't comfortable with that, I can skip that part."

"Are you kidding? That sounds like heaven." She opened the bag of chocolate chips, slipped a few morsels in her mouth, and closed her eyes on a small moan. "When I told Ollie we were staying here I mentioned it'd be like a little vacation. He was bummed you didn't have a pool, but I think I got the best end of this deal."

His blood turned to molten lava as he watched her enjoy her sweets. Maybe this wasn't such a good idea.

She patted the cushion beside her. "Sit."

Clearing the lust from his throat, he claimed the spot beside her then started the movie.

She shifted so there was space for him to sit behind her, her legs propped up on the couch. She swept her dark blond hair over one shoulder and exposed the long, slender column of her neck. Glancing behind her, she raised her brows and smirked. "Can't back out now."

"Wouldn't dream of it."

He scooted in so her body fit snug against him. "This okay?"

"Cozy," she said.

As the movie started, he squirted a dab of lotion on his hands then moved his fingers into her stiff neck muscles. "Is this too hard?" He didn't want to hurt her but wanted to apply enough pressure to help any lingering stiffness.

"Oh my God," she moaned.

Oh Lord. He'd made a mistake. A giant freaking mistake. Between her soft skin beneath his hands and the tiny sounds she made as he worked his fingers around her neck and shoulders, he might not survive.

At least not without an icy shower.

"It's been a long time since anyone's given me a neck rub," she said. "This feels amazing."

"Glad I can help. Hopefully you'll wake up feeling better in the morning."

He moved his hands down the right side of her back, pressing the pads of his thumbs into her flesh. His pulse thundered in his veins, and the minty smell of her shampoo drove him crazy. He wanted to press his lips to the sensitive spot behind her ear, to kiss the side of her throat, but he resisted the urge.

She'd kissed him earlier, but if she'd wanted things to go further, she wouldn't have pulled away. He understood and respected her need to take things slow. As much as he craved to devour every last inch of her right now, he'd hold back. Match whatever pace she took.

Even if it killed him.

The movie played on, but he had a hard time following along with the antics on the screen. He was too absorbed with every dip and curve he touched, the small mole at the side of her shoulder, and the way she melted further against him with each passing second.

The minutes flew by and her body went lax, her breathing heavy and even. Her head fell back and rested on his chest.

"Katherine?"

Nothing but a subtle snore answered him.

Indecision warred within him. The movie was close to finishing, and the hour grew late. He should wake her and tell her to go to bed. She needed a good night's rest.

Sighing, she curled against him, her hand resting on his side.

He wrapped his arms around her, and everything in his world shifted to perfection. The feel of her body on his warmed him to his toes, but it was the fact she felt safe enough with him to fall asleep that squeezed his chest. He'd wait a little while longer to wake her.

Shifting to recline against the edge of the sofa, he grabbed the remote and switched the television to a sitcom he'd seen a hundred times. His mind zoned out as the familiar cadence of the show lulled him into a trance.

He held Katherine closer, loving the feel of her even breaths against him. He'd give it another hour then send her to bed. Until then, he'd settle back and enjoy the way they fit together —revel in the feel of her wrapped safely in his arms.

12

"**M**ommy?"

Katherine blinked her eyes open at the sound of Ollie's confused little voice. Ollie's face filled her vision, his nose all but pressed to hers. His eyebrows dipped low. Fatigue and confusion muddled her mind. She tried to form words but came up blank.

She stirred against rock hard muscle, warm hands smoothed against the heated skin of her back. A steady *thump, thump, thump* beat against her ear. Sunlight streaked in through a window and nearly blinded her sleep-sensitive retinas.

Oh God.

"Did you and Cody have a party? You had chocolate!"

Bailey jumped up and down, her loud bark sounding as annoyed as Ollie.

Her heart shot up her throat, and she jolted upright.

Cody lay beneath her, slowly waking. He stretched his arms above his head and a sliver of abdomen showed, making her mouth water.

Down girl. Focus on the main issue.

"Mom." Ollie drew out the word into three whiny syllables. "I want candy."

"No candy for you, buddy. Give me a few minutes to get some coffee and I'll make you some breakfast."

Cody slid out from under her and stood, scratching the stubble along his jawline that was scruffier than usual first thing in the morning. "I got it. What do you usually eat? A T-bone steak? Beef burrito? Maybe lasagna?"

Ollie giggled. "No, silly. Eggs and toast."

"Oh, that's easy." Cody stretched his arms one more time, and when he dropped them to his sides, he looped one arm casually around Ollie's neck and steered him toward the kitchen. "How about you feed Bailey while I let her outside? Then your mom can take her time getting ready for the day."

"Mom doesn't need time. She's always pretty."

"Yeah, she is." Cody glanced over his shoulder and shot her a wink before opening the back door to let out a very excited Bailey. "You can scoop her food from that big container by her dish. Then she'll be ready to eat as soon as she comes inside."

"You sure you two are okay without me?" she asked.

Cody peered into the refrigerator and pulled out a carton of eggs. "We're fine. Go on and do what you need to do."

Katherine waited a beat to make sure Ollie didn't make a mess then made a beeline for Cody's bedroom. She closed the door and drew in a deep breath, but it did nothing to calm her frantically beating heart.

She'd spent the night with Cody. Wrapped in his arms. And Ollie had found them. She rubbed the heel of her hand over her tightening chest as she tried to come to terms with the sharp turn her life had taken.

But it wasn't a bad turn. She'd hoped Ollie would get along with Cody, and he'd been more upset he hadn't gotten chocolate than by seeing her with another man. Of course, at only seven, maybe he didn't understand exactly what he'd walked in on.

Which was what?

The most amazing night's sleep she'd had since Theo died.

She squeezed her eyes shut and pinched the bridge of her nose. So much for taking things slow, but she hadn't meant to fall asleep. Hell, the way his touch made her feel as he'd rubbed her neck, it was a miracle nothing more had happened.

Oh boy, she'd wanted it to.

But after a long couple of days and the comfort Cody provided, she hadn't stayed awake much after the movie started.

A grin spread on her mouth. She'd spent the night with Cody Hogan. Teenage Katherine would have been shocked as hell, but the young girl she used to be was an idiot to overlook such an amazing person.

She wouldn't make that mistake twice.

She still wanted to take things slow, but with Ollie seeming so happy to be around Cody and things progressing in such a natural way, maybe she could move along quicker than a snail's pace. She knew more than most that time was a luxury and she didn't want to waste any of it.

Huffing out a sigh, she crossed over the plush carpet to the bathroom. Decisions didn't have to be made today, or even tomorrow. Once things calmed down and she was no longer afraid for her life, she could really dissect her feelings—figure out what was best for her and Ollie.

The large showerhead in the middle of the shower caught her attention. The mom part of her brain told her to rush along, grab what was closest and get out to help in the kitchen. The other part told her Ollie was taken care of and enjoying the attention from Cody and Bailey. She could take a few extra minutes to take a hot shower and put herself together.

Decision made, she tested the water, ensuring it was warm enough to boil her skin before shedding her clothes and step-ping inside. She let the forceful drops hit the back of her neck and beat away the stiffness Cody had worked so hard to diminish the night before. Steam engulfed her, opening her pores and filling her lungs.

If time was a luxury, then a hot, uninterrupted shower was a downright miracle. Being a single parent the last year had taken so much of her—had changed the entire structure of her life. Since the day Ollie was born, she'd had a partner. A strong, wonderful man who doted on their son. Who made sure she had enough rest and was taking care of herself and not just Ollie.

But now it was all about Ollie. Her wants and needs simmered on the backburner, nearly turning cold with neglect. Even if her family had stepped up, it wasn't the same. Everyone focused their attention on Ollie—as they should—but she'd let parts of herself slip further and further away.

She'd have to fix that once the craziness of being hunted like prey ended. Life could go back to normal, and she could see how Cody would fit in her world. If it was as effortless and easy as the past few days—even with the chaos surrounding her—it wouldn't take much to open that door and let him in.

If that's what he wanted.

A little weight lifted from her shoulders, and she shut off the water. She stepped onto the cozy rug and dried off with the cotton towel hanging by the shower. She wiped the steam off the mirror with her hand and stared at her reflection. There wasn't enough time to dry and style her hair, but she could apply a touch of makeup and put on something that made her feel more like an attractive woman than a homeless lady.

When she was done, she tossed her towel into the hamper in the bathroom then padded out barefoot to the kitchen. She'd woven her long hair into a braid that hung over one shoulder and picked a long-sleeved blue t-shirt that hugged her just right. Not to mention leggings that tucked and lifted in a way that made her forget her pregnancy stretch marks.

She walked in on Cody and Ollie sitting at the table, flicking a folded-up piece of paper at each other.

"Touchdown!" Ollie scored and lifted his arms in the air. "Best breakfast ever."

Bailey barked in agreement.

Grinning, Cody glanced her way. "Yeah, buddy. Best breakfast ever."

LIFTING his second cup of coffee to his lips, Cody leaned back on the two-person glider on the deck and watched Ollie run around with Bailey. He pushed his feet against the wooden planks to move back and forth. A slight breeze rustled the air, and the sun shone bright in the vibrant blue sky. "Those two are going to wear each other out pretty quickly."

Katherine sat beside him with her legs tucked under her, cradling her own mug. "I doubt it. Ollie has boundless energy and doesn't stop until his head hits the pillow."

"Good thing Bailey's enough to keep him entertained," Cody said.

"Great," Katherine mumbled. "Now you've done it."

He frowned. "Done what?"

Ollie ran past the deck then doubled back around, squinting against the sun as he stared up at them. "So what are we doing today? I'm bored throwing the ball."

"You jinxed it," Katherine whispered under her breath.

"Oops. Guess I didn't know that unspoken rule." He wrinkled his nose and tried to think about something he could do to make both mother and son happy. "How about a walk? I own the land outside the fence. There are some pretty easy trails. A nice waterfall not too far away. Would Ollie like that?"

She grinned. "He'd love that. I planned to take him on a hike yesterday but with everything going on, it didn't seem like a good idea so we went to the shelter instead."

"Are you comfortable going now?" He didn't want her to feel unsafe about leaving his home. Even if they didn't venture far, she might feel better with doors to lock out any unwanted visitors.

"Seriously? As long as you're with us, I won't have a worry in the world." She stood then kissed his cheek. "I just need to put on my sneakers."

"I'll be waiting."

An ache pulsed in his chest as she disappeared inside the house. Damn, he had it bad.

Standing, he leaned against the rail to look down at Ollie. "Want to take a hike?"

Ollie jumped onto his tiptoes. "Really? Can Bailey come?"

"Oh, she'll insist on it. Do you want to grab her leash? She does okay without one, but if she sees a squirrel or chipmunk she might dart off. We don't want that."

"Where's her stuff?" Ollie asked as he stormed up the deck steps, Bailey on his heels.

"Her leash is hanging on the hook by the front door. Why don't you make sure she has some water before we go? Her dish should be filled, but if not let me know and I'll fill it."

"Okay." He zipped past Cody and ran inside, Bailey following. "Mom, I'm getting the leash."

His excited voice drifted out the open door and curved up Cody's lips. Having the little boy there brought so much energy into his house. He already dreaded the thought of Ollie not being around, but he wouldn't dwell on that now.

Katherine stepped outside and shook her head. "He's filling the water dish. I swear, at our house getting that kid to do anything resembling a chore is harder than pulling teeth. Here, he's hopping along, doing whatever he can to be helpful. Must be more of those tricks you were talking about."

He chuckled and set his coffee on the table then met her in the middle of the deck. He cupped her biceps in his palms, resisting the urge to wrap her tightly in his arms and kiss the hell out of her. "Boys love taking care of dogs. Maybe you should get him one."

"Ha! That's the last thing we need, and if you say anything like that to him there will be repercussions."

"So, what? You'll punish me?" A thrill shot through him as a dozen of dirty ideas of how that could play out sprang to mind.

She wiggled her eyebrows, her thoughts clearly matching his. "Maybe, but I have a feeling you might like that too much."

"No!" Ollie's yell from inside pulled them apart.

Katherine's eyes flew wide, and she spun around to dart in the house. "What's wrong? What happened?"

Cody was fast on her heels, crushing into her back as he spied the puddle of water under the upturned silver bowl.

Tears rimmed the corners of Ollie's brown eyes. "I tried to bring Bailey water. I'm so sorry."

Bailey stood beside Ollie, her ears perked and tail still.

Cody rushed forward and pulled the trembling boy in for a hug. "It's okay, buddy. It's just water. Trust me. Me and Bailey make much bigger messes than this. Do you want to help me clean it up?"

"You're not mad at me?"

The quiver in his words tore at Cody's heart. "Never. Now let's get some towels."

On his way to the bathroom, he caught sight of Katherine. Her own eyes glimmered with unshed tears, and she covered her mouth with her hands.

He stopped. "You all right?"

She nodded then shooed him away with a flick of a wrist.

Ollie ran past him. "I'll grab them."

He followed Ollie into the guest bath and plucked several large towels from the closet. He handed one to Ollie. "Use this one to start mopping up the water. I'll carry the rest."

They went to work cleaning up the mess and refilling Bailey's dish. When they were finished, Cody held the sopping wet towels. "See. No big deal. We all make mistakes, have accidents. It's all about how we clean them up that matters. Does that make sense?"

Ollive gave one big nod. "Yes!"

"And when we work together, we can clean things up even quicker. Now who's ready for that hike?" He held up his hand for a high five.

Ollie didn't disappoint. He slapped his palm against Cody's. "I am!" He sprinted outside with Bailey following close behind.

Katherine laid a hand on Cody's arm. "That was really well done."

Her compliment brought a rush of heat up the back of his neck. He didn't really have a ton of experience with kids, but it was easy with Ollie.

"I didn't overstep?" he asked.

"Not even a little bit. You handled it exactly how I would have—exactly how Theo would have. With understanding and a nice message wrapped up in a neat bow. Thank you."

"Anytime. We better get outside before they take off without us." He snatched the leash from where Ollie had dropped it on the floor and waited for Katherine to step onto the deck before closing and locking up behind him.

He wouldn't venture far from home, but he made sure to set the alarm before climbing down the stairs. "Here, Bailey."

The dog bounded to his side, and he attached the leash to her collar before handing the lead to Ollie. "You and the dog take the lead. Your mom and I will be right behind you. Just not too fast. We need to be careful on the trails."

"Sweet! This will be so much fun."

Katherine slipped her hand in his. "Ready?"

"One hundred percent," Cody said.

He didn't mean just for the hike. He was ready for her. He was ready for her son. He was ready to be whatever they needed him to be as they figured out the future.

13

Katherine couldn't be sure if Ollie didn't mind her holding Cody's hand because he was okay with having the other man around or if he was too distracted to notice. Either way, she would enjoy every second of this time together.

The canopy of leaves overhead blocked out the sun, but her long-sleeved shirt was enough to keep her warm. Especially at the brisk pace they kept as they traversed the uneven patch that snaked through a sea of trees.

"Slow down a little, bud," she called.

Ollie stopped for a second, glancing over his shoulder before taking off again, the leash he held tight from Bailey straining against it.

"That kid," she mumbled under her breath.

"Looks like we need to hurry up." Cody tugged her along.

"So much for a leisurely stroll through the woods." A break in the trees allowed beams of sunlight to shine through. She tilted up her face and let the warmth hit her skin. "I can almost believe that everything is right in the world. Almost forget the reason we're here."

"Let's pretend the only reason you and Ollie are here is to enjoy a day off. Thinking about all that other stuff will just bring us down and cause you to worry. It will all be there waiting for us when we're ready to dive in."

"I like that idea." She stared down the narrow trail. Ollie was nowhere in sight, and a beat of trepidation pulsed along with her heartbeat. "Is there anything around that bend I should be worried about?"

"Not for another mile or so, but we should catch up with Ollie before we get to the waterfall. It's a ways off the path, but I'd hate for him to try and get to it without us."

"You and me both."

Together, they hurried along the trail. A squirrel hopped from branch to branch overhead, and a chipmunk scurried around the forest floor beside them. The sound of the wind whistling through the leaves better than any symphony she'd ever heard.

With Ollie still not in view, she walked a little faster.

Frantic barking announced Bailey's distress seconds before the dog sprinted in their direction. The end of her purple leash bounced behind her.

"Oh my God," Katherine said. "Where's Ollie?"

She sprinted forward.

Cody shot out in front of her, grabbing hold of Bailey's leash as he ran. "Take me to Ollie, girl."

She didn't question if the dog had the ability to show them where her son was. She trusted Cody's instincts, and she knew that dog would only leave Ollie's side if she'd had no other choice.

Bailey barked and pressed her nose to the ground. She tugged at the leash, leading Cody off the dirt and into the woods.

Katherine stayed glued to him, scanning the area for signs of her son. "Ollie!"

"Mommy!"

Her heart raced and sweat dotted her hairline. She shouldn't have brought Ollie out here. Should have stayed locked up in Cody's house where no one could get them. If that sick sonofabitch who was after her got his hands on her child, she'd hunt him down and kill him.

Cody skidded to a stop on a patch of fallen leaves. He held out an arm to keep Katherine in place. "He's down there." He pointed toward the bottom of a steep slope.

"We need to get him!" Katherine lunged forward, but a strong arm around her waist locked her in place. "Get off." She slapped at Cody's hand.

"Mommy, my leg hurts," Ollie said, his voice a mere whimper. "I can't walk."

Cody clamped a palm on her shoulder and forced her to face him. "Just wait a second. He's scared and injured. You don't know this terrain, and I do. We don't need you to get hurt, too. Stay here with Bailey."

She didn't want to stay and wait. She wanted to charge down the ravine and get her son. But Cody was right. She didn't know this land like he did, and even once she got to Ollie, she'd struggle getting him back up the steep hill.

"Fine but bring me back my baby."

"I will."

She took hold of Bailey's leash and kept her focus trained on Ollie. "Cody's coming to get you, honey. Just stay right there. Don't move, okay?"

"I can't move," Ollie whined. "It hurts."

Bailey returned his pleas with whines of her own. She sat by Katherine's side, her feet pawing at the ground in little spurts as if she just waited for the signal to rush forward and help.

Katherine ran her fingers through her soft fur. "It's okay, girl. Cody's got him." She wasn't just uttering words to make the dog—or herself—feel better. She really meant it. There were few people she trusted her son with, and in a short time, she found Cody at the top of that list.

Time crawled by as she watched Cody pick his way down the hill. He maneuvered around fallen trunks and upturned roots. The space between him and Ollie grew shorter.

Katherine held her breath. Ollie didn't seem to be in distress, but there was no telling what could be wrong.

When Cody finally got to Ollie, a bit of relief loosened the tightness in her chest.

Cody cradled Ollie in his arms and trudged back up the hill.

Ollie clung to Cody, burying his face in Cody's neck. His leg hung at an awkward angle.

It didn't take a nursing degree to know something was seriously injured. Something that she couldn't fix at home.

Cody's mouth was set in a firm line, his face a mask of determination. He reached the top of the hill and kept on walking. "He needs a doctor. We should take him to the emergency room."

Panic swirled in her belly, but she called on all her training to stay calm. "Is it your foot or your leg?" she asked as she stayed in step beside Cody.

"I don't know," Ollie said between sniffles.

"Looks like his ankle, but I could be wrong. Nothing we can't fix, right buddy?"

"I'm sorry, Mom. I know I was supposed to stay on the trail, but Bailey ran after something, and I didn't want her to get lost. I held on real tight to the leash but then tripped and fell down the hill."

"It was an accident, honey. Just like the water," Katherine said. "Now we'll work together to fix it."

He responded with a pitiful cry. Guilt gnawed at her. This was a lot more serious than an overturned dog dish. Her son was injured and she couldn't fix him, which meant leaving their safe space.

She just prayed that getting Ollie the help he needed didn't lead them straight into more danger.

THE FEEL of Ollie's little body in his arms was imprinted in Cody's brain.

But now his arms were empty as he stood outside the room where the doctor examined Ollie.

He wanted to be in there. Holding his hand. Supporting Katherine. But it wasn't his place, and she hadn't asked. Better to stand guard and make sure no one lurked in the hallway, waiting to attack.

Heavy footsteps pounded on the linoleum floor, drawing his attention down the hall. A trio of pissed-off Wells men marched his way, Mike leading the pack.

Cody braced himself for impact.

"Where the hell's my grandson?" Mike barked.

"In the room, being examined."

Mike made a move to shove past Cody, and he took a step to block the door.

"Boy," Mike snapped out the word. "I suggest you get out of my way."

"And I suggest you take a seat in the waiting room until the doctor's finished and Katherine's ready for you come in."

Owen took a step forward. "Excuse me?"

Unintimidated, Cody lifted his chin. "Ollie's scared and his leg hurts like a bitch. Katherine's struggling to keep a brave face. The last thing either of them need is the three of you getting them upset. Give them a minute. Let her know you're here, and when she wants you to come in, she'll tell you."

Tommy rested a hand on Owen's shoulder. "Dude, calm

down. Cody makes sense. Katherine would be pissed if we just barged in there while the doctor was seeing to Ollie. Text her, give her a heads up we're here, and just relax. Both of you."

Appreciation relaxed Cody's rigid stance a fraction. At least he had one of them on his side.

Mike huffed out an irritated breath. "Well at least tell us what happened. All Katherine said in her text was Ollie might have broken his leg. You were supposed to keep them safe."

"We went on a hike. Ollie fell. It could have happened to anyone." He'd repeated the same thing to himself a thousand times, but he still didn't completely believe it.

Maybe it'd been a mistake for Katherine to stay with him. If she'd gone to her father's, Ollie would be laughing and playing, not sitting in a hospital room with a possibly broken leg.

Owen wiped a palm over his face. "Damn it. That's the last thing the poor kid needs. Why would you take them outside the house? Out in the freaking woods? My God, anyone could have been out there."

"Nobody was in my back yard," Cody snapped back. "We took my dog for a walk. I didn't send him flying over a canyon on a damn motorcycle. What were we supposed to do? Keep Ollie under lock and key until this all blows over?"

"No," Owen said, his voice low and taking a step forward. "But maybe do enough to keep my nephew out of the hospital. I wouldn't think that's too much to ask. Or maybe you were too busy panting over my sister to care about her kid."

It took every ounce of self-control to stop Cody from planting his fist in Owen's face. He didn't care if he was his boss or not. The bullshit spewing from his mouth was insulting not just to him, but Katherine as well.

The door behind him squeaked open, and Katherine squeezed through the sliver of space. "I'm not sure what's going on, but you all need to lower your voices. The last thing Ollie needs is to hear arguing."

Contrition pulled down the lines of Tommy and Owen's faces. "Sorry," they mumbled in unison.

Mike stood tall with his arms crossed over his chest. Anger and irritation and fear pouring off him in waves. "We wouldn't be arguing if Deputy Hogan would have let me in to see my daughter and grandson."

"Did you ever consider if I asked him to make sure no one came inside?" she asked, matching his defiant stance with one of her own. "That I wanted to focus on Ollie and only Ollie? Not managing everyone else's emotions when it's hard enough to regulate my own?"

Mike didn't apologize but he dropped his gaze to his feet.

Cody turned his attention to focus only on Katherine. He understood her family was upset and he was the easiest person to take it out on. But he couldn't get caught up in their bullshit.

He shoved his hands deep in his pockets. He wanted to reach out, to touch her and comfort her. But now wasn't the right time. Not with her family breathing down his neck and her afraid for her son. "How's Ollie?"

"Feeling better. I told him I'd grab him some hot chocolate while Jenna puts on his cast."

"I want to see him," Mike said.

Katherine aimed narrowed eyes his way. "You can wait. Jenna doesn't need you or anyone else hovering over her."

"Then what the hell am I supposed to do?" Mike tossed his hands in the air, his shoulders slumping forward.

Sympathy shoved aside Cody's earlier irritation. Mike was a man who wanted to take care of his family, keep them safe. His heart was in the right place, even if his actions pissed Cody off.

"Katherine's going to grab some hot chocolate while Jenna finishes with Ollie's cast," Cody said. "How about I go with her while you three find something for him in the cafeteria? I hear good things about the pudding."

Mike let out a long breath, as if relieved to be given a job.

"Yeah, Pops," Tommy said, slapping a hand on his dad's shoulder. "Pudding here's great. I might have to get some for myself while we're there."

Owen squeezed the bridge of his nose and closed his eyes for a beat. When he dropped his hand, he met Cody's stare head on. "We're not at our best right now."

Cody nodded then placed a hand on the small of Katherine's back to guide her to the vending machine. He might understand her family's overbearing ways at the moment, but he needed a second to catch his breath.

At the machine, he fished his wallet from his back pocket. "Do you want anything?"

Sighing, she leaned against him. "To be anywhere but here. Ollie was so brave, but I know his leg's hurting him. This is the first time he's been injured like this. I don't think I've ever been so scared."

Owen's earlier words crashed against him like a sucker punch. He'd loved having Ollie around but maybe he wasn't cut out for being any kind of authority figure to a kid. "I'm sorry I let this happen. I shouldn't have suggested that hike. Should have kept you both inside. If you want to head to your dad's, I'll understand."

"Are you serious?"

"I just want what's best for you two."

She flattened her palms on each side of his face and lifted herself onto her tiptoes. "What's best for us right now is to be with you. I feel it in my gut, and my gut's never wrong. Kids fall. They get hurt. That's life. But you swooped in and plucked him up and got him help. You did everything right, so don't beat yourself up. Don't let my family get inside your head."

Scrunching his nose, he rested his forehead to hers. "It's hard not to when they're all yelling at me. I can take it—will take it. And I even understand where it's coming from. I just don't know what all I should say. Don't know what this thing is between us to even explain it to them."

"This thing is new and exciting and no one's business but ours."

He grinned. "You make it sound so simple."

"Oh, it's far from simple." She let loose a small laugh. "It's messy as hell, but it's our mess."

Jenna popped her head around the corner. "There you are. I'm all done with Ollie's cast. He's eager for some signatures and I told him I'd find a cool superhero sticker for him. There's one in my office I know he'll love."

Cody fed his dollar to the machine and got the paper cup then hurried with Katherine down the hall.

"Knock, knock," Katherine said, stepping inside.

He lingered in the hallway, not wanting to intrude.

She glanced over her shoulder. "Come on in. We'll get the best spots for our names and piss off my family even more."

"Perfect." He entered the room, and his stomach sank at the sight of Ollie in the big hospital bed. Bright red scratches marred his face. "How you holdin' up, bud?"

"Good now. I've got this cool cast and a new stuffy. I think his name is Snitch. Maybe like Lilo and Stitch," he said, lifting his shoulders nearly to his ears.

Frowning, Katherine rounded the bed and ran a hand over the brown stuffed rodent of some kind sitting on Ollie's lap. "Did Grandpa bring you this?"

Ollie shook his head. "No. Some other guy. I think he works here, but he wanted me to have it."

Intuition tingled the base of Cody's spine, but he tried to keep the fear from his face. "Can I see it?"

Ollie handed it over.

Cody turned the fuzzy toy over and spied a name tag stuck to the fur. The word *Snitch* was written in large block letters, the same as the threat attached to the clock thrown into Katherine's living room.

He cleared all traces of emotion from his throat and handed the toy to Katherine. "Katherine, while you stay here with Ollie I'm going to find your brother. Lock the door behind me."

Understanding lit her eyes, and she pasted a tight smile on her mouth.

He fled the room then ran down the hall. Katherine's attacker was inside the hospital, and he had to figure out where he'd gone before he slipped right through Cody's fingers.

14

Cody's pulse raced faster with each barreling footstep down the wide, hospital hallway. He was looking for a man who could have slipped into Ollie's room unnoticed. Someone Ollie thought worked for the hospital.

A doctor at the end of the hallway turned in the opposite direction, and Cody picked up his pace. He ignored an irritated gasp from a female nurse who pushed an older woman in a wheelchair. He couldn't worry about proper etiquette right now.

He rounded the corner and closed the distance between him and a tall man dressed in blue scrubs. Reaching out, he grabbed the back of the man's shirt and yanked him backward.

"What the hell?" the man yelled and spun around, fists raised high.

The familiar face of Dr. Manning met him, and Cody took a step backward, shoving a hand through his hair. "Sorry. I'm looking for a guy pretending to work here."

"Sorry. I actually do work here and have a patient to see."

Cody glanced up and down the hall and spotted a janitorial

cart abandoned by the wall. He ran to it, peeking into the room beside it to see if anyone was inside.

Empty.

He studied the cart. A black-tipped marker rested on top of a crumpled sheet of waxy paper—the kind of paper peeled off the back of a name tag.

Shit.

A quick scan of the hallway showed a camera mounted in the far corner. He needed footage, and he needed it fast. He sprinted to the security office by the emergency waiting room.

Gus sat at the desk and kept an eye on the screens in front of him. He dipped his fingers into a glass dish and plucked out peanuts, popping them into his mouth as he watched.

"I need you to pull up footage of the south hall."

Gus turned around with a frown, his hand halfway to his mouth. "What?"

"South hall. Footage starting two minutes ago. Now." He moved into the room as he spoke.

Gus didn't ask another question, just pulled up what was requested.

A man dressed in a dark blue button-up shirt and matching trousers kept his head down and pushed a janitorial cart down the hall. He maneuvered it up against the wall, placed his hands in his pockets, and walked toward the exit.

"Just a custodian leaving his cart unattended. Probably had to use the bathroom or something," Gus said, continuing to munch on his snack.

Cody glanced at the time stamp than the clock on the wall. Less than ten minutes separated the moment the man walked away and now. Adrenaline pushed through his veins as he dashed back outside and headed for the exit the man had used —a side door that led to a smaller lot opposite the emergency room.

A black truck sped out of the lot seconds after he rushed through the door. "Shit." He reached for his communicator to call in the truck, but he was dressed in civilian clothes.

He nabbed his phone from his pocket just as Owen appeared in the doorway.

"What the hell's going on? Katherine's frantic, and Gus said you took off after seeing something on the security screen," Owen said.

"He was in Ollie's room. He just sped out of the lot." Cody jabbed a finger in the direction the truck had fled. "Where are you parked?"

"Other lot. I'll call it in and get more deputies to pursue. Tommy and I will jump in my cruiser. Get Katherine and Ollie to your house."

Cody followed Owen back inside, peeling off in the opposite direction. He jogged to Katherine's room, needing to be near her in case there was something he was missing. In case her attacker hadn't just fled the scene and still lurked nearby.

Katherine met him in the doorway, blocking Ollie from the conversation. "Did you find him?" she whispered.

He shook his head. "No, but Owen and Tommy are going after him."

Mike stood from a chair dragged up to the bed and marched their way. "Well?"

Cody repeated what he'd told Katherine.

"How the hell did this guy slip through the cracks?" Mike asked.

"Dressed as a janitor. He pushed a cart into the room, which is why Ollie thought he worked for the hospital."

Katherine pressed a hand to her stomach. "I think I'm going to get sick. He just walked right in here. He could have done anything to Ollie while he was alone. I can't believe I let this happen."

Mike snaked an arm around her shoulders and pulled her close to his side. He kept his gaze locked on Cody. "It's not your fault, honey."

The implication was loud and clear. But he didn't need Mike's accusing glare to make him feel bad. He already knew he'd let Ollie down, let Katherine down.

He swallowed hard, keeping his emotions from his face. "If Ollie's ready, we should leave."

"I still think they should come to my place," Mike said. "Especially now."

Katherine leaned against her dad, exhaustion clear on the contorted lines of her face.

For a second, he worried she'd agree. That she'd take her dad up on his offer and whisk Ollie off to stay with him.

Another part of him feared she wouldn't. What if he made another mistake? What if he let his guard down again and something else happened—something worse?

"Dad, we've already been through this. It makes more sense for us to be with Cody."

Mike worked his jaw back and forth. "I'll come with you then."

Cody tensed. He wasn't sure if Mike wanted to tag along to keep Katherine and Ollie safe, or to keep him away from Katherine. Either way, the idea of Mike sitting in his home, staring daggers at him the whole time, was less appealing than setting his own hand on fire.

"Yay! Grandpa's coming to Cody's house," Ollie chimed in from behind them. "He can meet Bailey."

So much for keeping the conversation away from the little guy's ears.

"Are you sure that's a good idea?" Katherine whispered. "Don't you want to be out there with Owen?"

"Being with you right now is the only place I want to be," Mike said.

Cody bit back a sigh. Having Mike in his house might not make him the most comfortable, but the older man needed to be with his child right now. He couldn't be the reason to separate him from his family.

"Your dad and I can do some more leg work while Owen and Tommy are out in the field. It'd be good for me to pick his brain a little. Maybe over some lunch."

"Yeah, I'm starving," Ollie said.

The exaggeration Ollie put on the last word made them all smile.

"How about I pick up your favorite meal at Lulu's, as well as food for the rest of us, and bring it over," Mike said. "Send me your address. I'll make sure I'm not being followed."

Katherine locked eyes with Cody, an unspoken question passing between them.

He gave a subtle nod. This might not be how he'd hoped to spend his day, but it was the right decision. Besides, maybe speaking with Mike about the case could shake loose some information because sooner or later, something had to give.

It had to, because Katherine's life hung in the balance.

KATHERINE PICKED at the soft bun on the top of her burger. She should be hungry, and the smell of her favorite sandwich from Lulu's tempted her to take a bite, but she feared her stomach would revolt. Between her frazzled nerves and lingering fear from knowing Ollie had been in the same room as a monster, food was the last thing she could handle.

"Not hungry?" her dad asked, frowning.

"Not really."

Cody carried a bottle of water to the kitchen table and took the seat across from her.

"How can you not be starving? We haven't eaten in hours." Ollie shoved a fistful of fries in his mouth as he spoke.

She mustered a smile for Ollie. No reason for him to learn how close he'd come to danger today. "That breakfast you and Cody made earlier must have filled me up."

Mike's bushy eyebrows shot up. "Ollie cooked?"

Ollie's chest puffed. "Yep. I'm a big help, right Cody? I even fed Bailey."

At the sound of her name, the dog's ears perked up, but she kept her head in Ollie's lap.

Mike snorted out a laugh. "Your dog seems pretty attached to Ollie."

Cody settled back in his chair, his own meal untouched. "The two have formed quite a bond. I'm pretty sure I've fallen to her second favorite person."

Ollie giggled. "Yeah, she definitely likes me more than you. She even slept with me last night, Grandpa. But that might have been because she couldn't fit with Mom and Cody."

Humiliation scorched Katherine's entire face. She might not care what her family thought, but that didn't mean she wanted her father to know where she'd slept last night.

Especially since that had been snuggled in Cody's arms.

Cody choked out a cough. "Hey, Ollie, I think Bailey needs to go outside. She was cooped up for a while. Do you want to finish your lunch on the deck? I don't think she'll go out if you stay inside."

"Sure. Come on, Bailey." Ollie braced his hands on the edge of the table to push himself up. "Can you help me?"

"Sure can." Cody retrieved the wheelchair they'd brought back from the hospital and pushed it to the table. He looped one arm around the little boy's back and helped him shift onto the chair then handed him the rest of his fries. "We'll be on the deck if you need us."

She waited for them to disappear on the other side of the glass door before meeting her dad's blank expression.

"What are you doing, Kat?"

She bristled at his hard tone. Her choices might be suspect to those on the outside, hell the things that had happened between her and Cody the last couple of days made her own head spin, but she wouldn't let anyone make her feel badly.

"I'm figuring out how to get on with my life," she said. "I'm not sure why that's so hard for everyone to understand."

"By letting your kid see you in bed with another man?" Mike threw his hand toward the door where Cody had disappeared with Ollie.

"First of all, we fell asleep on the couch watching a movie last night. Second, what I choose to do is none of your damn business. And if this is how you plan to act around Cody, you can leave." She shoved her burger to the side and crossed her arms over her chest. "I'm not a child and I refuse to be treated as one. I'm also a damn good mother and won't stand for you questioning my parenting."

Mike's face fell, and he rubbed the back of his neck. "Damn it all, that's not what I meant. It's just...this is all so out of the blue. I didn't know you and Cody were even friends and now this? And on top of everything else? How do you know it's not just a rush of emotion steering this ride? Shouldn't you slow down and wait until things go back to normal before making any big decisions? I just don't want you to get hurt."

Her heart softened. "I don't want that either, and neither does Cody. You're right. This thing between us is out of the blue, but it feels right. Feels easy and natural and I don't want to question it. I want to live it."

"And Ollie?"

She shrugged, wishing she had all the answers. "So far they get along. Ollie loves it here—Bailey might have more to do with that. But Cody's great with him. Theo would want us to be happy." Tears filled her eyes at the mention of her deceased husband.

The side of Mike's mouth shifted up. "I know that, honey. We all do."

"Then what's your beef with Cody? Because you, Owen, and Tommy have kinda been assholes. It's not fair. Cody's been great, taken all of your shit, and is still standing on that deck entertaining my son. If this progresses the way I hope, I don't want to be afraid to bring him around. At this rate, I think Pappy's the only one who's given him a fair shake."

Mike snorted. "I've really shit the bed if that old man is making me look like the bad guy."

Katherine grinned. "Something to think about."

"I'm sorry. I'm just worried about you and took it out on Cody because, well, I'm not really sure why. He's a good guy. A good deputy. I'll do better."

She reached across the table and grabbed his hand. "Thanks, Dad. I don't know what the future holds. Maybe it won't include Cody. But I want it to include happiness and joy and laughter. I didn't realize how much I missed that. Cody's brought that back in my life, in Ollie's life. I hope that continues."

Releasing her hold, she picked up her burger and took a bite. Melted cheese and tangy ketchup combined in her mouth, making her want another.

"After we finish, I'll take off," Mike said. "See if Owen needs a hand."

"I think you should stay."

"Really?"

She nodded. "Get to know him better. See him with Ollie. Plus I think he's getting antsy not diving into this investigation. Maybe the two of you can work together. As long as you promise to be nice."

"Not too nice." He shot her a wink. "You're still my little girl, even if you don't like it. I've got to make sure he's worthy."

She rolled her eyes. "It took you years to think Theo was worthy."

"He proved himself, and if Cody's the right man for you, he will too. Eventually."

Chuckling, she took another bite. Cody had no idea what he'd signed up for. Facing off against her father would either set them on the right path or send Cody running for the hills.

15

As much as Cody wanted to know what Katherine and her dad were discussing, he gave all his attention to Ollie. The two of them didn't need him hanging around while they hashed out whatever it was that needed hashed. It was better to keep Ollie entertained, something he found more enjoyable by the second.

Ollie traced his finger along the outline of the superhero on his cast. "Do you have any stickers?"

"I don't think so."

"That's too bad. The signatures are cool, but I want more fun stuff on my cast. I bet Jimmy has some."

"Maybe we can order some." He plucked his phone from his pocket and brought up a website that offered next day delivery. "Search for whatever you want."

Ollie's eyes grew wide. "Really? Anything I want?"

"Stickers only."

Ollie grinned. "Obviously."

The way he said the word made Cody think the kid would have had a field day if he thought he had free rein over his account. He offered the boy his phone. "Let me see what you pick before we buy anything, deal?"

"Deal!" Ollie grabbed the device, the screen quickly absorbing all his attention.

The door opened, and Katherine poked her head through. "Finished eating?"

"Yeah," Ollie said, eyes still glued on the phone. "Now I'm picking out stickers."

"Eyes up when speaking to me please," Katherine said.

Ollie glanced up.

"Explain."

"Cody said he'd buy me stickers. I get to pick them out."

Katherine aimed her raised brow his way. "You don't have to do that."

He shrugged. "I broke my arm as a kid. I wanted to decorate it and wasn't allowed. I had to draw my own designs on it, and none of them turned out cool. I understand the need to transform that hunk of plaster into something he's okay with looking at."

The tender look in her eyes warmed the hard pit that always formed in his stomach whenever he talked about his childhood. He wouldn't mention his father was the reason he'd gotten that broken arm in the first place.

"That's very nice of you, but you'll have to do it in a little bit. Right now, you need a shower."

"Oh, man. Can't I do that later?"

"No, sir. We should have washed that hospital stink off you as soon as we got back, but I didn't want your food to get cold. It might be tricky with your cast, so let's just get it over with. No arguments."

Ollie heaved out a dramatic sigh. "Fine. Can Bailey come?"

"Not a good idea," Cody said. "If she jumps in that shower with you, it'll take days to dry all that fur. She'll be waiting for you when you're done."

"How about you bring her inside?" Katherine asked.

Suspicion crinkled his eyes. "Why?"

"Dad's waiting for you in your office. He wants to go over some things about the case."

Her wide smile told him she was as nervous about that scenario as he was, but he couldn't refuse. Besides, if he planned to stay a part of Katherine's life, he and her dad should get a few things settled.

"I guess I'd rather take on your dad than get this one showered." He hiked his thumb over his shoulder at Ollie.

"Hey!" Ollie laughed.

"You'll be fine." Katherine squeezed his shoulder then rounded the back of Ollie's wheelchair. "All right, little dude. Let's go."

He waited for them to get inside before signaling for Bailey to follow and heading for the office.

Mike stood with his feet shoulder width apart, his hands locked behind his back, and staring out the window. "You've got yourself a nice place here."

"Thanks."

He turned to face Cody. "We have some work to see to, that's what's most important, but before we start, I want to apologize."

"There's no need," Cody said.

"There's every need. You've done nothing wrong and received the brunt of not only mine, but my sons', displeasure. We're all very protective of Katherine. I often have to remind myself she can take care of herself."

"Her grandfather says she's the toughest one of the bunch."

A puff of humor shot through Mike's nose. "That might be the only thing that old geezer and I agree on. She is tough, but she shouldn't have to be. As much as I want to make things easier for her, I don't have that power. But I can see how happy she is when she's around you. How at ease. It's scared the hell out of me."

Cody frowned, not understanding why that would be off putting for Mike. "Isn't that a good thing?"

A sad smile lifted his lips. "You'd think so, huh? But when you love someone so damn much and you've seen them endure unimaginable pain, you can't help but be fearful the good will go away again. That the bad times are waiting in the wings to steal her joy. That's not a way to live, but it's impossible to get out of your head."

Cody let his fingers drift through the fur at the top of Bailey's head and searched for the right answer. "I wish I could tell you I'll never hurt her, never cause her pain. But you and I know that'd be a false promise because life happens and we can't control so much of the shit that comes our way. What I can tell you is I'll do everything I can to keep making her happy —keep making all three of us happy."

Mike cleared his throat and swiveled back toward the window. "That's all I can ask for."

Bailey pranced over to Mike. She edged her nose into his hand.

Chuckling, Mile crouched and hooked an arm around the dog then scratched behind her ears. "She's a good girl."

Cody wasn't sure if he meant Bailey or Katherine. "The best."

"Well, that's enough of that," Mike said, standing. "I talked to Owen, and they had no luck tracking down that truck."

The news crushed down on Cody. He'd been so close to catching this asshole just for him to slip through the cracks once more. "Did he get a chance to go through the files I sent him last night?"

Mile frowned. "He didn't mention anything. What did you send?"

"I pulled up names of inmates recently released from the county jail. I started to cross check the names with their arrest records. Looking for anything that might pop out or point toward Katherine being involved in any way—even on the periphery. I didn't make much headway, so I sent the list along to Owen."

"He's had his hands full," Mike said. "Why don't you pull up the list and we can pour over it together. I mean, if that's okay with you."

Tedious research wasn't something he enjoyed. Something told him doing it with Katherine's dad would make the task even more laborious. But Mike needed to act, and he needed to further cement his relationship with the man who was so important to Katherine.

"It might take a while. You up for it?"

"There's nothing more important than finding the man harassing my daughter. I'll stay here all night if I have to."

Cody nodded and left the room to retrieve the computer he'd left in the living room the night before. He hoped he had one hell of a poker face. Last night had been heaven with Katherine sleeping in his arms. Tonight would be hell if her father chose to join them.

WITH THE DINNER dishes put away and her father finally gone, Katherine sat on the deck and watched Ollie figure out the best way to play with his new best friend. He couldn't run around the yard like he had the night before, but Bailey gently placed the ball in Ollie's lap after fetching. As though she understood the boy couldn't chase her right now.

Cody stepped outside with a full wine glass in each hand. "You said you like white, right?"

She smiled up at him. How was it possible to feel so damn lucky when her world was in such shambles? "I did. Thank you." She accepted the glass and scooted over in the glider to make room.

He sat, then took a sip before setting down his glass and circling an arm over her shoulders. "I needed something to take the edge off. My head is spinning after looking at all that data with your dad."

"You guys were at it for hours. Did you find anything?"

"I wish. I swear we looked at every person released from the county jail in the last year. We even started looking at recent arrests, thinking that the criminal potentially involved could still be incarcerated. We made some calls, did some digging, but came up empty every time. We can't find one thing that makes sense in connection with you."

Sighing, she leaned against him. "Can we put it away for the rest of the night? I just want to sit here and enjoy being with you—enjoy listening to Ollie giggling down there with Bailey."

He brushed his fingertips against the side of her bicep. "It's nice to hear him happy. He's not sullen or grumpy even after breaking his leg."

"You weren't the one who gave him a shower," she said, thinking back to the horror show cleaning her son had been.

"Fair point."

Questions brewed inside her like an impending storm. As much as she wanted to take her time with Cody and just enjoy what was happening between them, her life made that nearly impossible. She didn't have just herself to think about. There was a child involved, and his needs came first.

Always.

She couldn't dive in—or hell, even dip in her toes—to something new and exciting if there was no room for Ollie.

Tapping the tip of her finger against the edge of her wine glass, she debated the best way to broach a potentially difficult conversation.

Cody placed his free hand on top of hers, stopping her manic action against the glass. "What's going on in that head of yours?"

She glanced up, caught off guard by how the setting sun behind him made him look even more handsome. She should handle this delicately, slowly, but she couldn't find a tactful way to say what needed to be said.

"Do you want kids?" She blurted out the question then wrinkled her nose. "Sorry. I mean, when you've thought about what you want in your life, have kids been a part of that picture?"

Cody was silent for a moment, his attention fixed on the scene playing out on the yard. "Not really."

Her entire body recoiled. "Oh."

"No, I mean, I've never really thought about it before."

Pulling away, she glanced up at him and frowned. "How is that possible?"

He shrugged. "When I think about my own childhood, it puts a sour taste in my mouth. All the bad shit I went through makes me feel small, even now. It's pushed me to be the man I am today, to choose the career I have. But it's made me wary of what kind of father I'd be. I'd never want to put a child through the hell I went through."

The softness of his words hit her like an arrow straight through the chest. "I don't know your dad, but I know you're nothing like him."

"How can you be sure?"

"I've seen you with Ollie the past two days. You're kind and sweet. Firm yet gentle. You play and have fun with him but let him have his space when he needs it. He adores you."

"He makes it easy." Cody let out a sigh. "But what if I snap or lose control? What if something triggers something inside me and I scare him—scare myself. I mean, hell, I should have known better than to let him be so far in front of us today. I'm sure he wouldn't have taken that fall if he'd been with your dad or brothers."

Needing him to really hear her, she sat all the way up and

caught his face in her hands. "Being responsible for a child doesn't mean doing everything right or ensuring they never get hurt. It means doing your best every damn day to show them love. To give them guidance and provide the tools they'll need one day to make it on their own. I'm sorry you didn't have that with your own father, but it doesn't mean you can't be that person for someone else."

A hard pit formed in her stomach, and she turned away. Unexpected tears swarmed her eyes.

"Hey, what's wrong?" Cody unwrapped his arm from behind her back and shifted to face her.

"I...I don't know. It's just, talking about this reminded me of what an amazing father Ollie had. I don't want you to think I'm sitting here asking you to replace Theo. No one could do that." She shoved a hand through her long strands, struggling to pinpoint the myriad of emotions ping ponging through her body. "I need to make sure Ollie is as wanted as I am in any relationship I have. Oh God, I'm not saying we're in a relation-ship I only meant—"

It was his turn to cradle a palm against her jaw and force her attention his way.

She wanted to squirm under his gaze, to hide away and forget the word vomit she'd spewed all over him.

"I'd be lucky to have a kid like Ollie to hang out with, no matter what that looks like. I'd never try to be his dad or pretend like I'm more than what he needs me to be. As for me and you, we don't need a label as we figure this thing out. But as far as I'm concerned, this is a relationship. I mean, we're two people who care about each other, right?"

She grinned. "Right."

"And isn't that really what a relationship is?"

"You make it sound so easy," she said, throwing back the words he'd said to her earlier that day.

His grin matched hers. "It's only as easy as we make it. All you need to know is I'm here for you and Ollie. Kids might not have always been a part of my plan, but neither were you."

She laughed. "You mean you didn't dream about sitting on your deck with me while my kid and your dog play in the backyard?"

"Honey, never in a million years did I dream I could be this lucky. For once, my reality is so much better than anything I could have imagined."

"How do you do that?"

"Do what?"

"Always know how to say exactly the right thing to make me feel better? To settle my nerves and remind me to just take a breath and relax?"

The side of his mouth lifted along with one shoulder. "One of those tricks I mentioned."

Settling back against him, she couldn't help but wonder what other tricks he had up his sleeve and when she'd be lucky enough to discover them.

16

Cody rubbed the strain from his eyes then stretched his arms over his head. Between the time he'd spent with Mike and now when he'd snuck into his office while Katherine put Ollie to sleep, he'd stared at a computer screen way too long today.

Which would be worth it if he'd found anything to lead to an arrest.

Instead, he'd tracked down more released inmates from the tri-county area.

This investigation was starting to feel like searching for a needle in a haystack in the middle of sandstorm. But he'd keep poking and prodding to ensure Katherine's safety.

Katherine.

Just thinking about her made his heart stutter. He'd been naïve to think they could take things one day at a time without applying unnecessary pressure. She was a widow with a young son. Of course they needed to have the hard conversations before anything real happened. They couldn't chance hurting Ollie more than he'd already been hurt.

But was *he* ready? Ready to commit to a woman he'd hardly known a few days before—to a young boy who'd recently lost his father?

A tap on the doorjamb raised his eyes to the doorway. Katherine leaned against the frame, her head tilted to the side and long hair hooked over her shoulder. A pretty smile lifted her lips. "Still working?"

He closed the laptop and stood, drawn to her like a magnet. He rested his hands on her hips. "Not anymore. Ollie asleep?"

"Yeah. Didn't take much. He had a long day. Bailey's in there with him."

"I'd be more surprised if she wasn't." He grazed the pad of his thumb over her hipbone. "I'd suggest another movie, but that didn't turn out so well last night."

Her eyebrows rose high on her forehead, eyes wide. "Oh really? Sleeping with me was that rough for you, huh?"

The memory of her wrapped in his arms crashed against him, and he tightened his hold on her, drawing her forward until there was no space between them. "It was the best night of my life."

She swiped her tongue across her bottom lip. "You must not have had a lot of excitement in your life then."

"Oh, I've had plenty. What I haven't had is a beautiful woman I care so much about curled against me until morning. It's something I could get used to."

"Me, too." She rested a palm on his chest and rose onto her tiptoes, pressing her mouth to his.

He tried to restrain himself even as every nerve ending in his body was set on fire. He fisted her shirt in his hands, heat building in his core.

She opened her mouth, looping her arms around his neck to bring them closer. Her breasts pressed against his chest, and she darted her tongue over his.

A low growl rumbled deep in his throat. His restraint barely controlled on a very thin leash. He drowned in her taste, reveled in her movements as she deepened their kiss. He wanted more, wanted all of her, but dammit he was happy to have any part she was ready to give. "You're killing me, woman."

She nipped at his lip. "We wouldn't want that, but I do think we should maybe go somewhere a little more private in case Ollie wakes. I don't need him to tell my dad he caught us making out."

He groaned and rested his forehead on hers. His heart raced, his palms itching to touch more than just the soft fabric of her shirt. "Are you sure that's a good idea?"

He was stronger than he ever thought possible. At any other time in his life, her suggestion was all he'd need to swoop her into his arms and carry her to his bed. Keeping her there until they both needed food or water to survive.

But this was different—Katherine was different. His entire body screamed to charge full steam ahead, but his brain and his heart cautioned him to slow down. To take his time. To let her know he was okay with postponing the physical aspect of their relationship for as long as she needed.

Even if it killed him.

Taking a step back, she let her arms fall to her sides and frowned. "Sorry, am I being too forward? This is new to me. I just thought..."

The doubt he'd created played in the twisted expression on her face and tore him in two. "I want to make sure you're ready," he said. "I know if you keep kissing me like that, it'll be hard to stop. If you want to keep things light, for me to hold you like I did last night, then I need to step back and take a few deep breaths."

"All I want is you," she whispered. "All of you. Because you make me happy and give me hope for a future I never expected.

This is moving at lightning speed, but it feels right to me. I don't need to know where things are going or hear that you love me. I'm not a young girl with silly fantasies anymore. I only need to know that you want to be with me as much as I want to be with you."

Her admission broke something loose inside him. He pounced, capturing her lips again, he lifted her so her legs wrapped around his waist, her arms circling his neck. He backed her into the wall, kissing the long column of her neck while her heat surrounded him—intoxicated him.

With her head thrown back, her breaths lifted her chest and came out in ragged pants. Her middle pressed against him. "Okay," she said, the word a raspy whisper. "Bedroom. Now."

He didn't need to be told twice. He kept her firmly in his arms, his lips devouring hers, as he navigated down the hall and to his room.

She closed the door with her foot. "Got a lock on that thing?"

Struggling to find the lock, he reluctantly set her on her feet then twisted the function on the knob that would keep out all unwelcome visitors.

He turned toward her, and a feeling like he'd never had flooded his system.

She stood by the foot of the bed. Her hair a rumpled mess of wayward strands and her face flush and pink. Fire blazed from her hooded eyes.

"You're the most magnificent thing I've ever seen."

With her gaze locked on his, she found the hem of her shirt and pulled it over her head before tossing it to the floor.

The sight of her lacy black bra barely containing her full breasts snapped the leash on his self-control. He stalked over to her and cradled her jaw in his palm while he grazed the knuckles of his other hand over the subtle dip at her waist. Her skin was soft, a gentle vibration shaking her body.

"Are you sure?" he asked again.

"I've never been more sure in my life." She turned her face to kiss the inside of his palm then slid his hand down to slip the tip of his finger into her mouth.

In one swift movement, he hooked an arm around the small of her back and anchored her to his chest as they both fell onto the bed. He didn't know what tomorrow would bring, but for tonight she was his.

PLEASURE AND SATISFACTION combined in Katherine's body, making her bones melt against the soft mattress. She should look at the alarm clock and check the time, but then she might talk herself into going to sleep.

And sleep was the last thing she wanted, even though she wasn't sure she could handle any more attention from Cody.

Laying in his arms, she trailed her fingertip up and down his chest. Words escaped her as she struggled to catch her breath.

Cody trapped her hand with his against his hard muscle. "Are you okay?"

The question turned her to her side. Moonlight streamed in through the window and landed on his handsome face. She studied the subtle dip at the bridge of his nose and the hard line of his scruffy jaw.

He stared down at her, nothing but concern in his eyes.

"Of course I'm okay. More than okay. Why would you ask that?"

He brought her hand to his mouth and kissed her knuckles. "I told you before you can always be honest with me. Tonight's been magical, but I'm sure it's brought on more emotions for you. Maybe some things you hadn't expected. I just want to make sure you know I won't be upset if a part of you is grieving or even wrapping your mind around what just happened."

A tingle of emotion started in her nose, and she sniffed it back. Her eyes burned, and she blinked rapidly to keep any unwanted tears at bay. As much as everything about tonight—everything about Cody—was perfect, a part of her mourned something that she'd lost.

Even if she was thrilled at what she'd gained.

"It's hard to explain what's going on in my mind," she said, trying to find the right words. "I'm so happy. Beyond happy, really. But you're right, I can't help but think about how drastically my life has changed."

He tucked a strand of hair behind her ear. "I can't say I understand, but I do know there's no right way to feel. I'm sure this is hard for you."

She shook her head. "Nothing we did was hard. Well, almost nothing."

He let out a hoot of laughter. "Good thing or we wouldn't be having this discussion."

"Definitely no problems in that department." She smiled, enjoying the moment of levity. He made everything so easy—so natural. She didn't want him to think she regretted being with him, or that she'd let her past ever come between them. "It's hard for me to understand how I feel, let alone explain it. But it's like since connecting with you, my heart's grown in size to fit you in. Theo's still there and always will be. Having you here," she said, tapping her chest. "Doesn't mean I have to toss him out."

"No, you don't. As far as I'm concerned, he taught you the way you're supposed to be treated. Showed you how to be loved. As long as I'm in your life, it's my job to make sure I keep doing those same things, and if I slip, it's up to you to slap me upside the head and let me know."

"So now I get to slap you around, huh?"

"Only if that's what you like." He wiggled his eyebrows.

Now it was her time to throw back her head on a laugh. "We might need to ease into that."

Reclaiming her in his arms, he pulled her close to his side. "We have all the time in the world."

Sighing, she rested her head on the crook of his shoulder. She knew better than most that time was fleeting, but there was no need to point that out right now. In this moment, she wanted to focus on nothing but the good and exciting.

And boy was Cody exciting. Her body still hummed from the things he did to her. Her toes curled, and she ran her foot up and down his leg.

He groaned and swooped both arms around her, shifting so his long, lean frame pinned her to the mattress. "You're insatiable."

"Tonight I am."

He kissed her hard, his hand teasing her flesh as it moved up and down her torso. "I should set my alarm before we head into the next round."

She arched her back, every inch of her begging him for more. "Why, so you can time us?"

Chuckling, his warm breath tickled her ear. "Trust me, I have no desire to see how long this takes. But it's late and you're wearing me out. I don't want to fall asleep and have poor Ollie walk in on something in the morning that could traumatize him. I can get up early and head to the couch before he wakes."

His consideration for her son unlocked another level of happiness and she smoothed her palm against the side of his face. "Have I told you how amazing you are?"

"Not in so many words, but you've said so in other ways."

She kissed the smirk off his face. "I have a few more ways still to show you. You better set that alarm because once I'm done with you, you won't have the energy for anything else."

He messed with his clock then stalked over her like a hunter zeroing in for the kill.

A thrill shot through her. Giggling, she opened her arms wide as he dove toward her. She closed her eyes and let go of every thought clogging her brain, letting the man she was falling head over heels for take her to places she'd never been.

17

Daybreak streamed into the bedroom, rousing Cody before the screech of his alarm woke him. He reached over to fiddle with the clock, ensuring Katherine could get more sleep. He stared down at her, and longing constricted his throat.

Strands of messy hair were tossed over his pillow. The relaxed lines of her face made her look so peaceful. A light blush stained her cheeks, and her mouth was open just enough to let little breaths tickle the side of his neck.

He had to get up, because if he spent one more second in bed, he'd kiss her senseless. Just the thought flared the desire deep in his gut. Gritting his teeth, he kept himself in check and swung his legs over the side of the bed. He stood and found his joggers on the floor. He yanked them on then padded out to the living room.

A low growl sounded from the guest room. He hurried down the hall and popped his head in the room. Bailey stood at the end of the bed, her tail wagging like crazy. If Ollie woke without the dog in his room he wouldn't like it, but Bailey always had to pee first thing in the morning.

"Come on, girl. Be quick."

Bailey leapt onto the floor then dashed toward the back door.

Cody followed, letting her outside before she had an accident on the floor. He stood at the back door while she did her business, the cold, crisp air doing more to wake him than a cup of coffee. He breathed it in. The scent of the dew clinging to the grass better than any flowers.

"Mommy?" Ollie's voice floated down the hall and outside to Bailey's ears.

Bailey ran in and led the way back to the guest room.

"Morning, bud," Cody said, crossing the threshold. The curtain was pulled over the window and kept out the morning sun. "Your mom's still sleeping. Can I help you with anything?"

Ollie yawned and scooted up in the bed to a sitting position. "I'm hungry."

"I can fix that. Want to hop in the wheelchair or try the crutches?"

Ollie scrunched up his nose. "I'm too tired for crutches, but maybe after breakfast."

"Good idea." Cody secured the handles of the chair and wheeled it to the side of the bed then helped Ollie get situated. "Keep your hands and feet inside the ride at all times, please." He popped the chair back for a second then barreled out of the room.

"It's like a rocket ship," Ollie giggled.

Bailey stayed right in step with the chair.

Cody situated Ollie in the kitchen. "All right, little man. What sounds good this morning? We can do eggs again, or maybe bacon and pancakes? Cereal? Your pick."

Ollie swished his lips to the side. "What kind of cereal do you have?"

"I'm not sure. Let's check." Cody dipped into the pantry and found the limited options. He pulled out two boxes. "One with shredded wheat, one with little graham crackers."

"I *love* graham crackers."

"Easy enough." Cody bustled from the cabinet to the fridge then set a filled bowl on the table.

Ollie wheeled the chair over and grabbed the spoon Cody had set out. "Aren't you going to eat with me?"

"Coffee first." He ruffled the little boy's mop of hair before preparing his morning drink. Once the machine stopped hissing out steam, he filled a mug and sat across from Ollie.

Ollie propped an elbow on the table and rested his head in his palm. He dipped his spoon into the bowl then lifted it again, letting the milk drip off the end.

"Everything all right? Your leg hurt?" Cody wasn't used to seeing the boy so melancholy but couldn't blame him if he needed a few minutes to wake up.

"When do I have to go home?" Ollie kept his gaze fixed on the little brown squares in his bowl as he spoke.

"I'm not sure. Why do you ask?"

"I like it here. I don't want to leave you and Bailey."

Hearing Ollie's comment was pure bliss. When he'd offered his home to Katherine and her son, he'd figured it'd be something fun but also have its difficult moments. Times when he'd want his space or privacy, when the kid would be loud or off-putting.

That couldn't be further from the truth.

He dreaded the day he'd wake to find a quiet house with only him and Bailey. Hell, the dog would probably jump ship and find his way to Katherine's place so she could stay close to Ollie.

"Bailey and I like having you here," Cody said, not sure what else to say.

"Do you think I could stay forever?" Ollie finally looked up and tears rimmed his lashes.

The bottom dropped out of Cody's world. He wanted to say yes, to tell Ollie he could stay as long as he wanted, but he couldn't make those kinds of promises to the kid. At least not yet. "You can stay for now, and after you go back to your house, you can visit whenever you and your mom want."

One big tear slid down his cheek. "My house is sad. My mom's happy here. *I'm* happy here."

"Oh, buddy." Cody jumped from his seat and crouched in front of Ollie's chair. He gathered Ollie's hands in his. "My house is a much better place to be with you in it. Trust me."

"But you don't want me to live here?"

He squeezed Ollie's hands and said a quick prayer that he could find the right thing to say. "I want to hang out with you every chance I get."

Ollie chewed on his bottom lip. "But Bailey's going to miss me when I'm gone. Maybe she should come home with me."

Cody couldn't help but laugh. "She'll have to stay here. Then I know you'll want to visit."

Leaning forward, Ollie threw his arms around Cody's neck. "I'll always visit. Me and my mom."

Cody gave him a quick squeeze then returned to his chair and took a sip from his mug.

Ollie finally shoved a spoonful of cereal into his mouth. "Do you love my mom?"

Cody coughed, choking on his coffee. "Excuse me?"

"She seems to like you and smiles a lot when you're around. I saw her kiss your cheek yesterday. She used to do that to my dad. So does that mean she loves you like she loved him?"

A lump lodged in his throat. "It means we like each other and want to spend more time together. Is that okay with you?"

"Sure," Ollie said between bites.

The simple word loosened the stiffness in his neck that had tightened at the start of this conversation. He'd won over the most important person in Katherine's life. Now he didn't have one but two hearts to worry about.

And he'd do everything in his power to make sure both mother and son would never experience another heartbreak.

THE RING of Katherine's phone opened her eyes. A stab of disappointment pierced through her to find the bed next to her empty, but it was better for Ollie not to find Cody in here with her. She'd go out and find them in a second. First, she had to see who was calling so early.

Grabbing her phone, she spied Elsie's information before answering. "Hey."

"Good morning," Elsie said. "Just checking in. How are you doing?"

She smiled at the question. If Elsie only knew how well she felt this morning, it'd make them both blush. "Well, at the moment I'm great."

"You sound sleepy. Did I wake you? I didn't think you'd still be in bed at 9:30 in the morning."

"9:30!" She bolted upright and caught sight of the alarm clock on the nightstand. "Holy crap. Cody and Ollie have to be awake. I don't think Ollie's let me sleep past 8 am since he was born."

"Sounds like Cody's taking good care of you," Elsie said.

"Lady, you don't know the half of it." The words were out of Katherine's mouth before she could stop them.

"Oh really? I thought I'd call and find you scared and distraught. But sounds like you've been a little preoccupied."

She plopped back down on the mattress, the soft pillow cushioning her head. Memories from the night before flashed in her mind. She wouldn't share all the details with Elsie, but there was nothing wrong with a little girl talk with her good friend.

Besides, it'd be good to get Elsie's perspective on everything.

"Preoccupied doesn't even begin to describe the last few days. I'm really falling for this guy." She launched into a brief overview of the time she'd spent with Cody. "I'm still a little shocked with how quickly things have progressed, but I'm happy and really excited about where this could lead."

A beat of silence pulsed on the line.

"Elsie?"

"I think it's wonderful you're so happy, I just want you to be careful."

Katherine rolled her eyes. "Why is everyone so worried about this?"

"Maybe because four days ago you hadn't said more than five words to Cody Hogan since high school."

The stark reminder was like a punch in the gut. "True, but that doesn't lessen the way I feel about him. He's been wonderful with Ollie and gone out of his way to help me. To take care of me. He's kept my mind off all the horrible stuff that's happened."

"Could that be one of the reasons you've thrown yourself into this relationship? I mean, it's not really like you to jump in with both feet before carefully weighing every single aspect. Especially when it involves Ollie. I mean, have you even made a pro/con list?"

"Hey, don't make fun of my lists. They help me make a lot of important decisions."

"And have you made one for Cody?"

"I don't have to. I know what my heart is telling me."

"And it has nothing to do with being distracted from reality? You've taken a lot of heavy hits. First with Theo and now this. Is there a part of you that wants to pretend like everything is rainbows and butterflies for a little while?"

Katherine hated the hard slap of truth from her friend. Her dad had said something similar—about letting the roller coaster of emotions take over instead of thinking things through. She sighed, hating that the perfect little bubble she and Cody had created the last few days might be popped.

"I suppose my feelings could be a trauma response. Clinging to the dopamine and forgetting the chaos. Maybe I've gotten caught in a fantasy that's too good to be true and I'm using Cody to avoid reality."

The door swung open, and Cody stood in the hallway. He rubbed the back of his neck, his gaze fixed at the floor. "Sorry. Didn't mean to disturb you. Ollie needs to use the restroom, and I figured it'd be better for you to help him."

"Oh, okay. I'll be right there."

Cody kept his head down and walked away.

"Shit," she whispered.

"What is it?" Elsie asked.

"I think Cody overheard that last part. He came into his room to let me know Ollie needs me and when he left, he looked like a broken-hearted little puppy dog."

"You're in his bed?" Elsie screeched. "You conveniently left that part out of the conversation."

Katherine cringed. "I've got to go. Thanks for checking in. I'm fine, Ollie's fine, and now I need to smooth over whatever mess I might have made." She disconnected before Elsie could get in another word.

Jumping from the bed, she found her robe and wrapped herself in the soft terrycloth. She dashed out to the hallway.

Ollie sat in his wheelchair, his body jostling up and down. "I really got to go."

She looked for Cody, but he was nowhere in sight. She'd deal with him later, first she had to see to Ollie.

Once her son was taken care of, she hurried to the living room with Ollie. "Where's Cody?"

Ollie shrugged. "I don't know, but can I watch cartoons with Bailey?"

"Sure, honey." She fiddled with the remote until she found something she approved of then went in search of Cody.

He sat at his desk in the office, the computer open and his focus fixed squarely on the screen. He didn't so much as glance up when she stepped inside.

"Good morning. Thanks for letting me sleep in. I haven't done that in years."

A tight smile stretched across his mouth. "No problem."

She clasped her hands in front of her. Dang it. Last night had been so special and now she'd gone and accidently put her foot in her mouth. "Was Ollie a handful?"

"Not at all."

Awkward silence lingered between them and she'd do anything erase it. "Are you working?"

"Yeah."

"Same stuff you were researching with my dad?" She scraped her thumbnail against her skin, hating the tension covering the room like a wool blanket.

Sighing, Cody finally glanced up. "I pulled more data. We focused our search on Cooper County and got nowhere. I'm expanding the radius. We know someone is angry with law enforcement and for some reason thinks of you or someone close to you as a snitch. My gut says I'm on the right track. I just need to focus and stay on task."

"Oh, okay. I won't disturb you then." She turned to walk out of the room.

"Katherine, wait."

She stilled, agony pressing down on her lungs. She faced the door, not wanting him to see the hurt she knew would be so clearly written on her face.

"If you aren't sure about what you feel for me, I'd appreciate if you tell me first. Honesty is the most important thing."

She spun around. "It's not that I'm not sure, it's just that so much has happened in so little time. I'm afraid that when the danger is over, this thing between us will die with it."

His stone-faced stare didn't bely a single emotion. "Then maybe we should take a step back before someone gets even more hurt. Once you're safe, you can figure out what exactly it is you want."

She swallowed past the sadness lodged at the base of her throat. "I know that right now I want you. Isn't that enough?"

The lines on his face softened. "It would be if your son hadn't asked me this morning if he could live here—if he hadn't wondered if we love each other."

She closed her eyes. Ollie was so invested. But what did she expect? She'd tossed her son into this whirlwind situation without a second thought as to what it could do to him.

"I don't need to know if you love me," he continued. "I don't need to figure out where I stand in all this. But there's too much on the line for you to mistake your feelings—for you to leave my home and realize I'm not enough for you."

"I'd never think that." She took a step forward, wanting to erase any hurt she'd caused this man who'd been so amazing.

He held up a hand and gave a tiny shake of his head. "Please. Stop. We don't know how long this will continue, and I can't stand the idea of falling even harder for you only to discover it was all a lie. A way for you to cope with the evil outside these walls."

Her heart broke into a million tiny pieces, but she nodded. Before she broke down, she walked away and shut the door to the office behind her. In the blink of an eye, she'd not only compromised her entire future, but crushed the man who'd brought her so much joy.

She didn't need the nightmare lurking outside to end to know she'd just made a huge mistake. One she may never recover from.

18

S itting at his desk, Cody squeezed the bridge of his nose and second guessed every decision he'd ever made. Because every choice led him to this moment, with the woman of his dreams and her adorable son in his home while he barricaded himself in his office.

The ache in his chest was so raw, so real he could barely breathe. He'd been so transparent, so open with Katherine. He'd thought she'd been the same, but he was the biggest fool of them all.

Teenage Cody would laugh at the idea of Katherine Wells giving him a second look. Maybe he'd had it right all those years ago.

The letters in front of him blurred together and he shut the laptop. He needed a break—needed some fresh air.

Hell, who was he kidding? He needed Katherine.

He pushed back his chair to stand, but his ringing phone sat him back down. He swiped the device off the desk and answered. "Hogan here."

"Hey, man. It's Tommy. Mind if I stop by?"

Cody frowned. "Are you sure that's a good idea?"

"I've got some photos to show Katherine."

"Can't you email them?" Having Mike come over the day before was a big enough risk. He didn't need a whole parade storming around his property and drawing unwanted attention.

"Nope. I have prints."

Cody straightened. "Of what?"

"Dad stayed up all night searching through the files you pulled. He found an arrest from three years back, someone Katherine went to high school with. That guy's still in prison, but it's the only connection we've found so far."

"What'd he go down for?"

"Assault with a deadly weapon. He claimed self-defense, which was bullshit since his wife was beat to hell. Katherine cleaned her up at the hospital."

Cody let loose a low whistle. "Awful lot of coincidences. But who'd be the one holding the grudge if the husband's still behind bars?"

"Guy comes from a family of assholes. You know how it goes. The whole damn tree is poisoned, ruining every apple on it."

The sentiment made Cody's stomach drop. Yeah, he understood how a family name could haunt you, drag you down to hell.

And never let go.

"I've got photos of some of the family members for Katherine. A couple from a yearbook. A newspaper clipping with the guy's dad. Even an uncle. All have served time, and I wouldn't be surprised to see them lashing out on behalf of their relative."

"Then looks like you asking if it's ok to stop by is a bit of a moot point."

"Sure is, especially since I'm pulling in your driveway. Besides, I didn't get a chance to sign Ollie's cast."

Cody grumbled under his breath and disconnected before

stalking across the room. He yanked open the door and his gaze instantly found Katherine's.

She sat on the couch with Ollie tucked beside her, Bailey on the boy's other side.

His stomach muscles clenched and he wanted nothing more than to storm to her side, sweep her into his arms, and tell her to screw everything he said. To go back to enjoying each other as much as they could for as long as they could.

But what he said was important. She had to know where her heart lay before he went any further. For Ollie's sake and his own. He'd already fallen hard. Any harder and he'd crash and burn.

A knock on the door widened Katherine's eyes. "Who's that?"

"Tommy. He has some things for you to look at."

Katherine dropped a quick glance at Ollie before meeting Cody's eye again. A hundred questions shone from her irises.

He wished he had answers for her, but hopefully after their visit with Tommy, at least one issue could be settled. He continued to the door, opening it wide.

"Hiya, bud." Tommy slapped a hand on his shoulder and walked past him into the house.

Bailey barked and hopped off the couch, greeting Tommy with a wagging tail and lolling tongue.

"Hey, girl. Good to see you again," Tommy said, running a hand over the top of her head. "I bet Ollie loves being around you."

"Uncle Tommy!" Ollie spun around on the couch and grinned. "What are you doing here?"

Tommy wiggled a black marker in the air. "I have a cast to sign. Amelia wants to sign it too. I told her maybe in the next couple of days."

At least Tommy had enough sense not to bring his and Sadie's daughter to the house. The last thing Cody needed was another child running around while trying to keep his head on straight.

Katherine stood and walked to her brother. She gave him a quick hug then stepped back, her arms wrapped around her waist.

Tommy frowned. "You okay?"

She shrugged. "It's just been a lot."

"It's been a lot for a few days and you've been in better spirits than I've seen in a while. Something happen?"

Katherine kept her gaze down and shook her head. "Must be tired."

"Sorry, sis." Tommy looped an arm around her shoulders. "We'll nail this guy and everything will go back to normal. I promise."

The promise was enough to rip Cody's heart from his chest. He didn't want normal, he wanted new. The thought of returning to the lonely and isolated hours he thought he preferred made a cold sweat break out at the back of neck.

But this wasn't about him—at least not entirely. Katherine had to figure her shit out, and apparently, she needed real life to start back up before she understood her feelings for him.

And dammit, that hurt like hell. All he needed was one look, one touch to be sure where his feelings for her stood. But as much as he wanted to shout that from the rooftop, to urge her to believe in him and them and everything they could have together, she had to sort through her emotions herself.

He wouldn't beg. Wouldn't coerce or manipulate a woman to love him.

Love.

His breath caught at the base of his throat. Where the hell had that word come from? Yes, he was certain beyond a shadow of a doubt his feelings were strong and real. But love? Was it possible to fall that hard so fast?

Katherine glanced his way, and the truth smacked him in the face.

No matter what she decided, she held his entire heart in his hand. He loved this woman, and there was nothing he could do but give her the space she needed.

And pray she didn't crush him in the process.

SITTING at the kitchen table without Cody felt like Katherine was missing a limb. Okay, more accurately like her arm had been sawed off and someone waited in the wings to slam her upside the head with it.

She'd made him feel like he wasn't enough.

Agony sizzled inside her like burnt butter. They'd spent the most amazing night together—after a whirlwind few days that left her breathless and happy—only for her to let everyone else get inside her head.

She *knew* her feelings were real. *Knew* she wanted a future with Cody. And now instead of clearing things up between them she was staring at photographs in Cody's kitchen with her brother.

Her skin itched to jump up and find Cody and talk, but that had to wait. He'd taken Ollie outside so her son wouldn't overhear all the details Tommy needed to share.

"Does he look familiar?" Tommy asked.

She struggled to focus. This was important and deserved all her attention. She picked up the weathered newspaper article and squinted to bring the man in the photo into better focus. "No, I'm sorry." She tossed the paper back on the table. "Who is it?"

"Eric Rider's dad."

She winced at the name of the man Tommy had told her about. She'd never met him, but his wife had left a lasting impression. The battered woman was one of the reasons she'd decided to volunteer at Safe Haven Women's Shelter. The poor wife had suffered at the hands of her abusive husband for years, feeling trapped and like there was no one there to help. Her story had haunted Katherine, prompting her to give back and help others who found themselves in similar situations.

"You really think that guy's dad would track me down because his son was arrested for beating his wife?"

Sighing, Tommy shoved a hand through his shaggy hair. "Weirder things have happened. What about his brother?" He flipped open a yearbook to an earmarked page and pointed to a surly teenager with pimply skin and close-cropped hair.

"When is this yearbook from?" she asked.

"Five years ago," Tommy said.

"Well, this guy doesn't look familiar, but he could have changed a lot in five years. But again, I think it's strange he'd be so hellbent on avenging a monster of a brother."

Tommy shrugged and flipped the book closed. "Families stick together. If the dad or brother thought their blood was wrongly accused, they may want to make things right in their own way."

She thought of Cody's family. Of the hell he'd survived with a criminal as a father and brother. "Not all people fall into the same bad habits as the people who raised them."

Tommy cringed. "Shit."

"What?"

"I said something similar to Cody on the phone—some crap about bad people from bad families. No wonder he's in a pissy mood. I should apologize. I really do like the guy, Kat."

"He's a good guy." Tears sprung up and choked off her sentence.

"Hey, what's wrong?" Tommy slid his hand over to cover hers. "I can put all these pictures away if this is too much for you."

"That's not it," she said, waving away his concern. "I messed everything up."

"With Cody?"

She nodded. "I had a moment of doubt, and he overheard me say some things on the phone. Now he thinks I need to take time to sort through my feelings before we go forward with anything."

"Okay. That doesn't sound like a bad idea to me. I mean, you've been through a lot. Then you two were thrown together and things happened so quick. Allowing both of you to have some space to really analyze things could be a good thing."

"I don't need time to understand my feelings. After Theo died, I thought that part of my life was over. Cody's reawakened parts of me I'd buried along with my husband. I lo—" Gasping, she covered her mouth with her hand. She widened her eyes and stared at the comically shocked expression on her brother's face. "Holy shit."

"Holy shit is right," Tommy said. "I'm not the one you should be saying this to. We both know that tomorrow isn't promised. Don't waste a single second of it. Talk to Cody."

Nodding, she rubbed at her aching chest. "I will. Maybe tonight when Ollie's asleep."

Tommy squeezed the hand he still held. "No. Now. I'll hang out with Ollie. I'll clean this up then head outside."

Fear shot through her, but she pushed it down. She couldn't be afraid to take hold of the life she wanted—the life she deserved. And that started with being vulnerable with Cody.

"Thanks, Tommy." Standing, she pressed a kiss to her brother's cheek then made a beeline for the backyard.

Bailey ran in a large circle around the fenced-in back yard.

Ollie laughed and threw a tennis ball, clapping his hands as the dog let the ball hit her in the face then bounced after it in the corner of the lawn. "She's so silly!"

Cody chuckled. "That's why I call her a dufus."

"Hey, you two, I hate to break up the fun, but Tommy and I are finished. He wants to come out and play with you and Bailey for a little bit if that's okay."

"Bailey will love that," Ollie said.

Cody turned for the deck steps. "I want to have a word with him really quick. Keep throwing that ball or Bailey will freak out."

As he passed her, Katherine grabbed his shirtsleeve. "Can that wait? I'd love to have a conversation."

Uncertainty danced in his eyes. "Let me get this out of the way first, then we can talk. If that's what you want."

"I need to talk, and I need you to listen. You know, every woman's ideal situation." She winked to let him know she was teasing.

A small half-smile cracked through his gruff expression. "Sounds about right."

"Be quick." She resisted the urge to press her lips to his, something that had become as natural as breathing.

He dipped his chin then jogged the rest of the way inside.

"Mom, come watch Bailey," Ollie said. "She doesn't know how to catch a ball."

Pasting on a wide smile, she erased the distance to where Ollie sat in his wheelchair. "All dogs know how to catch tennis balls, silly."

"Uh-uh." Ollie shook his head. "Watch."

He tossed the ball high in the air.

Bailey jumped up on her two back paws, her nose sniffing in the air as if trying to find the ball. The ball whizzed toward the ground and bopped her on the head. She barked, bounced around like a lunatic, then chased down the ball before carrying it back over to Ollie.

"See," he said on a giggle. "She can't catch."

Katherine couldn't help but laugh. She'd feel bad for the pooch if Bailey wasn't standing with what could only be described as a smile and a wagging tail. "Maybe you threw it up too high. She likes to chase it better. Throw further for her so she can run more."

"Okay." Ollie drew his arm back and hurled the ball like a missile.

Bailey raced forward but was forced to stop at the fence and watch the ball land amongst the trees. She leapt up and down, barking like crazy.

"Oh, no. Mom, you have to grab the ball," Ollie said. "She might jump over the fence and run away. Hurry!"

Although the dog had a great vertical, Katherine doubted Bailey could get her doggy butt all the way over the black wrought-iron fence. But the worry in Ollie's voice hurried her to the gate. "All right, but then we'll go back to teaching her how to catch. I'm not the one supposed to be playing fetch."

She unlatched the gate and made sure to close it behind her. The last thing she needed was Bailey following her and getting lost, defeating the whole purpose of her coming back here in the first place. Fallen leaves crunched at her feet and the sun disappeared as she stepped between the large trees.

The snapping of a twig reached her ears and sent her heart racing. Goosebumps erupted on her arms and the hairs on the back of her neck stood straight up. Screw the ball. Cody had more in the house. He could come get this one later.

She turned to hurry toward the house. A hard grip on her arm pinned her in place.

"Not so fast," a man said, his deep voice shooting bile up her throat. "You're staying here with me. Don't try to run. I wouldn't want to hurt your little boy."

19

A gun.

The man had a gun pointed straight at her.

Katherine's world stilled, her heart lodged in her throat and mind worked in overdrive. She raised her hands in the air as she faced her attacker. He wore military-style fatigue pants with a stained tan T-shirt. Wrinkles along his brow told her he was older than she was, maybe middle aged. He wore his hair short, and a full beard covered the bottom of his face.

Not one tingle of recognition rang inside her.

"I don't want you to hurt anyone," she said, hoping to take his attention off Ollie.

He tilted his head to the side, and a twisted smile curved his cracked lips. "Isn't that funny. You don't want me to hurt anyone, but you had no problem using your power to ruin other people's lives. Seems a bit hypocritical, don't you think?"

"You have the wrong person. I didn't ruin anyone's life, at least not on purpose. I don't even know who you are."

Bailey barked non-stop from where she stood on the other side of the fence, nearly drowning out her own thoughts.

The man huffed out a humorless laugh. "Shocking. Too

self-absorbed to even know the chaos you caused. It's a good thing I'm here to set things right."

Her brain went into overdrive, trying to both decipher who stood before her as well as how to get away from him. She might not know the woods outside of Cody's house well, but the path they took the day before was to her left.

Which meant the ravine Ollie fell down wasn't far away.

If she could make a run for it, she could get down the ravine and hide. Her phone was in her pocket. She could call Cody, and he'd find her. It might be a long shot, but it could work.

The man tapped the gun against the side of his head. "I can see those wheels spinning. Not a good idea to try and come up with some stupid-ass plan."

Refusing to show her fear, she inched up her chin. "Why not? You think I should just do whatever you tell me? Accept my fate without even trying to fight back?"

"You can try, but then I might have to put a bullet in that poor, helpless kid. The way these two trees part, I have a perfect shot. He'll never see it coming."

An icy terror like she'd never known flooded her system. "Please," she said, her shaking voice belaying her every emotion. "I'll do whatever you want. Just don't hurt him. He's a little boy. He's done nothing wrong."

Begging for her son's life broke her heart in two and created a soul-deep hatred for the man standing in front of her. She'd never been a violent woman. She'd always believed communication created understanding. But right now, all that bullshit washed away, revealing a mother who'd rip anyone to shreds if they hurt one hair on her child's head.

But she had to keep her cool. One misstep wouldn't just put a bullet in her head, but potentially one in her son's as well.

"As long as you do what I say, I'll leave him alone. But one wrong move and I make no promises."

"Just tell me what to do. I swear," she said. "I'll do whatever you say."

"Glad to see I've gotten your attention." He reached into one of the pockets on the side of his pants, pulled out a red bandana, and tossed it her way.

She snatched it out of the air.

"Tie that around your eyes. I don't want you seeing where we're going. I'd knock you out but hauling your ass to my truck would be too much trouble. But first, toss me your phone."

Her hands trembled as she handed over the phone then hooked the fabric around her face. The smell of stale cigarettes and sweat threatened to activate her gag reflex. She was tempted to tie the bandana in a way that she could catch a glimpse at where this man was taking her. But she couldn't risk doing anything to upset him.

At least not with Ollie so close.

A hard yank on her elbow pulled her forward. She tripped over her own feet, struggling to stay upright as she was dragged along. Twigs snapped and leaves crunched with each step. Her mind spun as she tried to figure out which direction she traveled.

Time was an illusion. Her heartbeat the only sound in her ears. Her compromised vision messed with her senses, and it took every ounce of will power to put one foot in front of the other. When she stepped on loose stone and the heat of the sun beat down on her face, her fear spiked to a new level—they were out of the woods.

The energy around her shifted, and the feel of her captor's body next to hers made her want to recoil. But she stood tall, refusing to let him see how shaken she was.

"Now that we're by my truck, I don't have to worry about keeping you awake."

She opened her mouth to scream, but something hard smashed against the side of her head. Her body crumpled to the ground and her eyes slid shut as one thought played on repeat in her mind.

At least Ollie's safe.

~

LEANING OVER THE TABLE, Cody glanced through the photos Tommy had brought by for Katherine to see. "You really think one of these guys could be who we're after?"

"Hell, I don't know, man. Seems like a long shot, especially since Katherine didn't recognize either of them. But we're grasping at straws."

"Anyone call them? Check for alibis?" Cody asked.

"Owen's on it now. I figured if I could get a positive ID from Katherine, it'd give us more ammo for Owen to use. No luck there, but that doesn't mean we're off the mark."

Cody tossed down the photo. "Doesn't mean you're on it either."

"By the way," Tommy said, reorganizing the papers and placing them in the folder. "Sorry about what I said on the phone earlier—that crack about the family being bad or whatever. I didn't mean anything by it."

Cody snorted. "Trust me. That's the least of my worries right now."

A knowing grin spread on Tommy's face. "My sister can be a real pain in the ass sometimes, but don't let that scare you away. I think you two would be good together."

It took some self-control to not react to him calling Katerine a pain in the ass. Instead, he zeroed in on the other part of his sentence. "You do? Hasn't really seemed that way."

"Yeah, well, I was caught off guard." Tommy shrugged. "But you're a good guy. Always have been. You and my sister just kinda click. Don't let her push you away because she's scared."

Cody sighed. He was about to have this conversation with

Katherine. He didn't need to have it with her brother. "When all this shit passes, the fear can go away. Maybe it'll be easier to know where things stand then."

"Dude, it's not all this shit that she's afraid of." Tommy waved a hand over the file resting on the table. "She's scared of being hurt. She's gone through hell the past year. A type of hell I never want to experience. But she survived. She doesn't want to go through that kind of loss again."

"And the first time she waffled even a little about her feelings, I all but shoved her out the door. Son of a bitch. What the hell was I thinking?"

"Probably that you're a little scared too, but don't worry, I won't say a word." Grinning, Tommy winked. "You'll be fine. If being with Sadie has taught me anything, it's communication fixes all kinds of mistakes. That and flowers. Always bring home flowers."

Urgency rushed through his veins to fix his blunder and make things right. He'd reassured Katherine they could take everything at whatever speed she was comfortable with, and the first chance he got he pushed her too far and made her feel badly. Damn, he was an idiot.

Not wanting to waste another second, he headed for the back door he'd left open when he'd stepped inside moments before.

"Mom! Hurry up!" Ollie yelled.

Bailey's incessant barking urged Cody to run outside. Crisp air skimmed his cheeks, and he lifted his hand to shield his eyes against the blinding sun.

Ollie sat in his wheelchair on the lawn. He shifted his body back and forth, bracing his palms against the armrests to lift himself a little in the air as he looked out to the woods beyond the fence.

Bailey stood at the gate. A low growl rumbled from her throat.

Katherine was nowhere in sight.

"Ollie, where's your mom?" he asked and jogged down the deck steps.

"I threw the ball over the fence. She went to get it and hasn't come back yet. I don't know what's taking her so long."

Terror sat heavy in his gut as he raced across the grass. "Tommy, get outside now! Stay with Ollie."

He didn't wait for a response as he swung open the gate and charged into the dense cover of trees.

Bailey stayed beside him, her nose pressed to the ground.

"Katherine!" he called, feet pounding through the dense foliage and searching for any sign of her.

Nothing but the sound of Bailey's labored breath and birds chirping overhead answered. He stilled, turning in a circle to scan the area. A round green ball caught his attention, and he sprinted to the tennis ball.

He wanted to charge through the forest and track her down, but he had no idea which way she went. Fear tightened like a noose around his neck and cut of his breath. His mind spiraled higher than the white, puffy clouds as a dozen worst case scenarios spun in his head.

No, he couldn't go down that path. He had to act—had to call in Owen and every other deputy at his disposal and find Katherine.

Sprinting back to the yard, he found Tommy standing at the gate. His eyes were wide, mouth pressed in a tight line. "Where is she?"

"She's gone. Call your brother. Whoever took her has a head start. We need to move fast."

Tommy grabbed his phone and made the call.

"Cody?"

Ollie's scared little voice almost brought tears to his eyes.

He walked over to the boy and crouched in front of him.

"Where's Mom?"

"I don't know, buddy."

"Does the bad man have her?"

Dear Lord, how could he look this boy in the eyes and answer his questions honestly without breaking his heart?

He grabbed Ollie's hand and squeezed. "I think so."

"Are you going to find her?"

"I'm going to do everything I can to bring her home. I promise."

Ollie threw his arms around Cody's neck, his tears soaking through the fabric of Cody's T-shirt.

As much as he needed to get moving, he held the boy tight for a minute longer. He didn't take his promise lightly. He'd move heaven and go to hell and back to bring Katherine home. Not just because Ollie needed his mom, but he needed the woman he loved.

20

Awareness trickled through the darkness holding Katherine hostage. Throbbing pain in her head beat along with her pulse, turning her stomach and forcing her eyes closed. She groaned and curled onto her side. Maybe if she lay here long enough everything would go back to normal. Her world would shift to the way it was supposed to be, and she'd wake from this nightmare.

But wishful thinking wouldn't get her out of this mess.

She opened her eyes and light blasted against her retinas. Her stomach revolted and the throbbing against her temples turned into body-consuming agony. She slid to the side of the bed and let her head fall over the edge seconds before vomit spewed from her mouth.

Heaves wrecked her body, sweat dotting her hairline. After she emptied her stomach, she wiped her mouth with the back of her hand then flopped back on the mattress.

Oh God. She was laying on a bed.

A different kind of terror shot through her and forced her to a sitting position. She leaned her back against the dirty wall and took in her surroundings. The bare mattress she sat on was pushed against the far corner of the room. An old dresser with a missing top drawer was the only other furniture. The carpet was thin and stained.

But one fact reigned supreme in her mind.

She was alone.

Ignoring all her pain, she shoved up to her feet and staggered toward the closed door. She lunged for the handle, but when she turned it, the door wouldn't budge.

Shit. She was locked in. There had to be another way—another option. She wouldn't just sit around and wait for her abductor to come and do whatever it was he had planned. Patting her pockets, she searched for her phone but came up empty. Disappointment pressed down on her lungs. She'd handed that over before putting on that stupid bandana.

Okay. No phone. Doors locked. Look for something else to help.

She spotted the lone window on the other side of the room. A threadbare curtain blocked out most of the sun. Pulling in a steadying breath, she made her way to the window, praying she could wiggle her way out without being noticed. She peeled away the fabric and found a fifteen-foot drop.

She swallowed hard. The fall could kill her but so could staying in this room. A large maple tree was close to the house. If she could jump far enough, she could grab hold of a branch and climb down to safety.

From this vantage point, there weren't any neighbors, but she wouldn't waste time figuring out what to do until she was free. First, she had to get to that branch.

Leaving the curtain in place as much as possible, she found the lock and clicked it over then yanked at the ancient window. Splintered wood scraped against her fingers and the house groaned with the effort it took for her to get the glass to budge a fraction of an inch.

The muscles in her arm screamed from the strain, but she kept trying.

Exhausted, she dropped her arms. A tiny breeze whistled inside the crack, but it wasn't even wide enough to fit a finger let alone her whole body.

She blew out a long breath, steeled her nerves, and went back to work. More groaning and creaking as the window moved little by little.

The sound of footsteps made her heart gallop. The opening still wasn't big enough. Her brain screamed to keep trying, but logic told her if her captor found her attempting an escape, it wouldn't end well. She tore herself away from the window and reclaimed her spot on the mattress. If she closed her eyes and pretended to still be passed out, maybe he'd leave her alone.

Curling into a ball, she evened her breathing and let her eyes drift shut.

The door squeaked open. Footsteps grew closer. The energy in the room shifted, and dread coated her skin.

A hard slap across her face made her body snap to attention, her arm instinctively covering her cheek to ward off another attack.

"You think you're so smart, don't you?" He spat out the question. "I could hear your footsteps downstairs. I know you're awake."

Her eyes squeaked open, but her body stayed still. She stared up at him and willed her mind to remember his face. Maybe if she could place him then she could figure out how to talk herself out of this mess.

Or at least buy more time until Cody found her.

Cody.

Her entire body ached with longing at the thought of him. She had so much faith in him, so much trust. How could she have made him believe she didn't? She had to get out of here alive because she had to make things right with him. She couldn't die letting him think she didn't love him.

Then there was Ollie.

Tears stung her eyes.

No. She couldn't go there. If she let her mind wander to her beautiful son, she'd fall apart.

"There she is," the man said. "Welcome back. I hit you a little too hard. Bet your head hurts like a bitch."

"Why are you doing this?" she asked.

"Because you need to be taught a lesson. You took away the last fifteen years of my life. You ruined me, then went on like nothing happened. Didn't even realize how much damage you caused. All because you couldn't keep your fucking mouth shut." His temper rose with each word until his shouting rang in her ears.

Fifteen years? What the hell happened fifteen years ago that resulted in this man trying to kill her?

"I was seventeen years old at that time. Just a kid trying to figure out the world after my mom died. I never hurt anyone."

"You hurt me." His arm shot down like a striking snake and he grabbed a fistful of hair, yanking her to her feet.

Her head screamed and a cry broke through her lips. "Please. Please stop."

He twisted her strands in his hand and brought his face inches from hers. "And now I'm going to hurt you. Nice and slow. I've waited so long for this—thought about it every damn day while I rotted away in that jailcell."

If she hadn't already emptied her stomach, she'd have thrown up. But she couldn't crumble. Couldn't just let him do whatever he wanted while she cried and begged for mercy.

Adrenaline pushed through her blood and blocked out all the pain. She had too much to fight for. She would not be a victim. She lifted her hand and jabbed her fingers into the man's eyes, pushing as hard as she could until he released her hair.

"You bitch!" He took a step back, dropped his gaze to the ground and shielded his eyes with his hands.

She jabbed an elbow to his nose, forcing his head back up as blood quirted from his nostrils. Taking a step forward, she jammed her foot down on his then rocketed her knee into his crotch.

Groaning, he fell to the ground.

She sprinted toward the door and found herself in a narrow hallway with stairs at the end. She ran toward the staircase and leapt down the steps. The stairs spilled into a bare living room, but the sight of the brown walls and spindled railing stirred a memory.

Shocked, she inhaled a sharp breath as she made a beeline for the exit. She knew exactly where she was, but one question still remained.

Why?

~

CODY STOOD in the kitchen surrounded by Katherine's family. Guilt and fear ate away at him.

If only he'd had the conversation she'd asked for right then. Or if he'd insisted she and Ollie come inside so they weren't alone.

But he hadn't. And now she was gone.

"I spoke with Eric Rider's dad, brother and uncle," Owen said. "All have alibis. They don't have her."

"Which leaves us with diddly shit," Mike said. He stood with his arms anchored over his chest. His face a tight line of torture. He flipped through the papers wedged in the file Tommy had brought and scattered them around the table. "We have to be missing something."

Anxiety crawled over Cody's skin. He wanted to be out in the world, pounding the pavement and knocking on doors. But there was nowhere to go, no tracks to follow. He and Tommy had gone through the woods and found no trace of Katherine or the person who'd taken her. It was as if she'd vanished.

But that wasn't possible, and time was running out.

Elsie sat in the living room with Ollie. She'd tried to get him to leave but the boy refused. Not even the promise of time spent with Jimmy could coax him from the house where he was convinced his mother would return.

Tommy paced, biting his thumbnail. "Let's go over everything we know again. Maybe something will stand out this time."

Cody squeezed his eyes shut and replayed everything they'd learned. "The person we're looking for has an axe to grind against authority and a personal vendetta against Katherine. Called her a snitch, so he thinks she told on him or is the reason for something bad that happened. No one who's been released from the Cooper County jail in the past year fits the bill, and the list of released prisoners from the tri-county area is a mile long."

A light hand on his shoulder opened his eyes, and he found himself staring into Elsie's kind eyes. "I'm not a cop, but I've had my own brush with danger. When my roommate was kidnapped it's because she stumbled into a crime by accident. Could something like that have happened to Katherine?"

He shoved a hand through his hair and tried to recall all the conversations he'd had with Katherine. "Nothing she mentioned to me. Do you guys remember anything happening a few years ago, or hell, longer?" He tossed the question to her dad and brothers.

Owen and Tommy shrugged.

"Not really," Owen said. "Katherine wasn't one to get into trouble. Even to just stumble across it. She was always with Theo. The two of them usually stayed home or did pretty boring stuff. Movies, football games, the usual."

Tommy let out a small, nostalgic chuckle. "We always joked they were already an old married couple even as teenagers."

A smile cracked through Mike's gruff expression. "She was the easy one. Took on a lot of responsibility after her mother died. Not like these two knuckleheads who I always had to worry about."

A tingle of an idea nagged the back of Cody's brain. "We talked about that. She said after her mom died, she rebelled a little. Went to a couple of parties but it left a bad taste in her mouth. She didn't elaborate much on what happened, though."

Owen's expression hardened. "I remember that. Her friend Donna Jo took her to some college party. I wasn't happy when I found out about it, but glad Katherine made the right decision and left. She was pretty shaken up about it."

Something shifted in Mike's eyes. He dropped his arms to his side and worked his jaw and forth. "Wait a second. You called and told me about it right after Katherine got home. She was upset and didn't want me to know she'd snuck off somewhere she wasn't supposed to go. But she thought her friend had been slipped something and drugs were being passed around like candy. And didn't she struggle to get her friend to leave because she was afraid she'd be taken advantage of if she stayed?"

"Yep, sounds about right. Thank God Katherine knew better than to drink while she was there. That night could have ended a lot differently," Owen said.

Elsie shook her head. "So many bad people doing bad things in this world. I hope they got in trouble."

"I didn't have any jurisdiction over there, but made a call," Mike said.

Cody's eyes flew wide. "Would that be public knowledge?"

Mike frowned. "What?"

"That you, sheriff of Cooper County and Katherine's father, was the one who made that call?"

"I don't see how," Mike said. "Unless someone there knew who Katherine was. Understood her connection to law enforcement so assumed she was the reason for the police showing up."

"We need to find out what happened that night," Cody said. "If any arrests were made, and if so, if anyone put away that night has recently been released. What county would that be? Holms?"

"Yeah," Mike said, grabbing his phone from his pocket. "She was at a house party near the college. A little outside of town so the sheriff's department would have handled it. Let me make a call."

A beat of hope pulsed through him as a new theory took form. Maybe Katherine couldn't remember what she'd done to wrong someone because she hadn't known the wheels she'd set in motion.

But someone did. And they had to figure out who before it was too late.

_____

21

While Mike jumped on the phone, Cody rounded the sofa and sat next to Ollie. As much as he loved having the boy close, it'd be better for him to leave with Elsie. There was no telling what lay ahead, and he needed to be shielded as best as possible.

"Did you find my mom?" Ollie asked, eyes wide and filled with fear.

"Not yet, buddy. But we might have gotten one step closer. Your grandpa, uncles, and I will leave soon to track down some leads. I think you should go home with Elsie until this is all done."

Tears slid down Ollie's cheeks. "I want to stay with you."

The statement yanked at his heartstrings until they were pulled all the way off. "I wish you could but that's not possible. I need to focus on your mom right now, and I can do that better if I know you're safe with Elsie."

"What about Bailey?" Ollie rested his head on top of the dog's. "She shouldn't be alone."

Elsie joined them, standing behind the couch. "You know, I

think Jimmy would love to meet Bailey. If Cody's okay with it, she can come with us."

Ollie still didn't look convinced, but he swished his lips to the side in consideration. "Will you call me when you have Mom?"

The fact that he said *when* and not *if* buoyed Cody's own hopes. "I will."

Ollie heaved out a sigh. "Okay. I'll go with Elsie."

Cody gave the boy a big hug and kissed the top of his head. When he stood, he fought his own tears from falling. "I'll see you soon."

Forcing himself away from Ollie, he slipped into the guest room and packed a bag for Elsie to take. He prayed Ollie would be back in his own bed tonight but there was no telling what the coming hours would bring.

A bright flash of pain slammed against him so hard his vision wavered. He wanted this room to be Ollie's, wanted the bed covered in a superhero blanket and toy cars scattered on the floor. Hell, even stepping barefoot on Legos sounded like heaven.

He hoped to make that vision reality, but before that could happen, he had to bring Katherine home.

With Ollie's stuff in hand, he waited for the boy to say his goodbyes to his family then helped Elsie get Ollie and his wheelchair in her car. When everything was loaded, he stood in the driveway and waved goodbye as he watched them leave.

He turned around and found Mike standing on the front porch.

"He means a lot to you, doesn't he?" Mike asked.

"They both do, sir."

Mike nodded. "Then let's find Katherine so the three of you can put this nonsense behind you. I spoke with the Holms County sheriff. We were able to pinpoint when Katherine was at that party, and she pulled some files. They made a big bust that night. A drug dealer was using some frat as a way to traffic product and he happened to be at that party. He was put away for fifteen years. Released a month ago."

"That's got to be him," Cody said. "Do you have a location?"

"I have an address," Mike said. "Lives about ten minutes from here. Near the county line between Cooper and Holms."

Owen and Tommy poured out of the house, determination clear in every stride.

"I'll drive," Owen said.

Cody hurried to Owen's cruiser and climbed inside. He sat in the back with Tommy, leaving the front seat for Mike.

Owen settled behind the wheel and took off.

"What all do we know about this guy?"

"Name is Keith Stiller. Age forty-seven," Tommy read off his phone. "One previous arrest prior to the one that put him away for fifteen years. Here's a photo." He tilted the screen toward Cody.

Recognition tightened his stomach muscles. He was transported back to the night this asshole grabbed Katherine at the hospital. To the night his world had changed forever. "Son of a bitch. That's him."

Owen turned on the siren and lights. "Call this into the station, Tommy. Dad, call your contact at Holms County Sheriff Department. The more backup we can have, the better."

While they went about their assignments, Cody plugged the address into his phone and found a layout of the house. He studied the exits, the arrangement of the rooms. He memorized every inch by the time Owen cut the siren.

"We're almost there," Owen said. "No need to alert him to our presence. What's the plan?"

Cody handed his phone to Mike. "Here's the layout. Two exits. The front door feeds right into the living room. A side door goes into the attached garage. Kitchen and bathroom on the first floor. Three bedrooms and a bathroom upstairs."

"Me and Cody will head to the front door, Owen and Tommy through the side," Mike said. "We go in with weapons drawn. Owen and Tommy, clear the first floor while we head upstairs. We get my baby girl out of there, got it?"

Owen parked the car in the driveway and all four men hurried out.

Cody secured his gun and released the safety. He took the lead, running up the cracked sidewalk with Mike behind him, Tommy and Owen going to the garage.

He tried the handle, shocked when the front door swung open. He glanced over his shoulder at Mike. "Ready?"

"Hell yeah."

Steadying his nerves, Cody stepped inside. Musty, stale air greeted him along with the hum of appliances. He noted the sound of Owen and Tommy entering the house as he pounded up the stairs—Mike right behind him.

Nothing but silence lingered in the hallway, but he couldn't focus on the fear that brought along with it. He opened the first door and stepped into an empty room. Disappointment dipped his gut. He stepped back in the hall as Mike stepped out of another room.

"Nothing," Mike said, frowning.

Cody went to the third door and pushed it open. The same sight greeted him. An empty room, the closet door pushed open.

He met Mike back in the hall. "Anything?"

Mike shook his head. "Doesn't even look like anyone lives here."

Cody rushed back downstairs only to find Owen and Tommy with matching pissed-off expressions.

"No sign of her," Owen said. "Are you sure this is the right house?"

"It's the address the sheriff gave me. She got it from his

parole officer." Mike braced his palms on either side of his head. "Where the hell are they?"

Cody struggled not to fall to pieces as time ticked by. The longer Katherine was missing, the more likely she was hurt or worse. But he couldn't go there—couldn't get caught in the quicksand of worst-case scenarios.

"I'll call the parole officer." Mike nabbed his phone from his pocket. "See if he has any other ideas where Keith could take Katherine. Family, friends, place of work. Anywhere."

An idea took root in Cody's gut. "What about the house where he was arrested?"

Narrowing his eyes, Tommy cocked his head to the side. "What do you mean?"

"Criminals return to the scene of the crime all the time. If Keith is determined to make Katherine pay for her part in his arrest, he could take her back to where it all began."

"It's better than anything else we have to go on," Owen said. "The house shouldn't be too far from here."

"It's not," Mike said. "The address was in the police report the sheriff sent over."

"Send it to me," Owen said.

Not wanting to waste a second, Cody ran outside. He had one more shot at getting to Katherine. He just prayed he wasn't wrong.

KATHERINE COULDN'T STOP and figure out why this man had brought her to some house she went to one time as a teenager. Hell, it didn't really matter. All that mattered was getting as far away from him as possible.

Feet separated her from the front door. She grabbed the handle, and a gunshot blasted through the air, a bullet lodging in the splintered wood of the doorframe.

She dove to the floor and covered her head with her hands. Pain rippled through her.

"You think you can just run out of here? That I won't keep chasing you?" The man staggered down the stairs. A slight limp slowed his progress, and blood flowed down his face. He aimed the gun at her, the weapon bouncing in his unsteady hand.

"Just leave me alone," she screamed, frustration boiling inside her. "I don't even know who the hell you are."

He stopped and scratched his chin with the barrel of the gun. "You don't remember the last time you were here?'

"Yes, but what does that have to do with you?"

"You left here and ran to Daddy. Told him everything that was happening, and he sent the cops after me. I was arrested that night and thrown in jail. I lost my business and my freedom. I lost fifteen years of my life in that hellhole. All because of you."

He aimed the weapon at her again, and she curled into a ball. The coldness from the linoleum seeped into her skin. Maybe if she just laid here and took the bullet meant for her, it'd end her quickly.

He continued down the stairs. "Maybe once I'm done with you, I'll go back for the boy. I missed out on my own kid's life, and now she wants nothing to do with me. It's only fair I repay the favor."

Something inside of her snapped. She could take her share of abuse, but the moment her son was threatened she had no choice but to fight back. He was already battered and weak. She just had to get the gun away from him before he used it on her.

She needed to keep him talking.

Raising to her feet, she kept her palms in the air. "I'm sorry for your troubles," she said, the apology bitter on her tongue. "But I never told my dad about that night. I wanted to forget it ever happened. I was scared of what I saw at that party and terrified I'd get in trouble if my dad found out I was there."

He sneered. "You think I believe that? You're just trying to save your own ass." He heaved out a labored breath and leaned against the railing of the staircase.

"I promise. I had nothing to do with it." She wouldn't add that if he was selling drugs to teenagers, he deserved exactly what he got. Something told her that wouldn't help her case. "If the police showed up, it wasn't because of me."

"Lies!" he screamed, the gun bouncing even more in his grip. He was feet away.

It was now or never.

She channeled every ounce of fear and anger and frustration and catapulted herself forward. She wrapped her arms around the man's waist and slammed him to the ground. They bounced down the rest of the stairs and landed in a pile on the hard floor.

The gun blasted against her eardrum. Pain ripped into her side. She shoved it away and scrambled for the weapon.

The man struggled under her, squirming and bucking until his body pinned her into place. Laughing, he shoved the weapon in his waistband and circled his hands around her neck. He applied pressure, stealing her breath. "This is much better. Now I can see the life leaving your eyes."

She clawed at his hands and twisted her body to get him off. Her strength leaked from her system. Dark spots dotted her vision and her raw throat labored to bring in air to no avail. Tears leaked from the corners of her eyes.

This couldn't be how it ended. Away from everyone she loved on a dirty floor, a madman's face the last thing she saw before taking her final breath. She had a son who needed her. She had a life waiting for her.

She had Cody.

An image of Cody holding Ollie in his arms crept into her mind's eye. She clung to the picture, urging it to stay in focus. To stay with her as she edged closer to death.

In a flash, the man pinning her down was off her, his hands no longer around her throat. Was this death? Had everything around her floated away as her soul left her body?

"Katherine, stay with me honey. Look at me. Take a breath. Please, baby."

Cody's pleas reached her ears, and she gasped against the fire blazing a trail through her neck. She blinked open her eyes and stared up into the most beautiful baby blues she'd ever seen. "Cody?" The name was so sweet on her lips even if it hurt like hell to speak.

He cradled her in his arms and smoothed a palm along her jawline. "I'm right here. You're going to be okay. I promise."

Commotion caught her attention from behind Cody. Owen slapped a pair of handcuffs on the man who'd tried to kill her and dragged him to his feet. "She did a number on you, huh?"

The man growled but hung his head.

Her dad grabbed a fistful of the man's hair and forced him to meet his eyes. "You're lucky my son's the sheriff. If it was just me here, I'd kill you for hurting her."

Tommy rested a hand on Mike's shoulder. "Come on, Dad. Let Owen get him in his cruiser. We need to call an ambulance for Kat."

She rested her head against Cody's chest and winced as pain vibrated every nerve ending in her body.

"Katherine, you're bleeding." Urgency came through Cody's words, but she couldn't bring herself to care. The bad man was going away, and she was back with the man she loved. That's all she needed to know.

"Honey, I need to know where you're hurt. Help's on the way, but if there's something serious happening, I need to figure it out. Can I lift your shirt a little?"

She wanted him to stop talking. To just hold her tight while she closed her eyes and got some rest. "So tired," she murmured.

Cool air touched her skin and gentle fingers moved around her torso.

"Shit, she's shot," Cody said. "How long before medics get here?"

"Just pulled in," Tommy said.

More commotion. More people. Someone swooped in and took her away from Cody—away from his warmth and comfort.

"No," she said, reaching for him. "Don't leave me."

As she was loaded onto a stretcher, Cody stayed beside her and grabbed her hand. "I'll never leave you, Katherine. Now you promise me the same thing, okay? Don't leave me now. We have way too much to look forward to. An entire life together."

A small smile lifted one side of her mouth. "That sounds nice."

Her eyes slid shut and all her pain fled. Peace settled into her bones as she welcomed the darkness, her hand going limp in Cody's.

22

C ody sat next to Katherine in her hospital room, her hand sandwiched between his. Machines beeped beside the big bed where she lay with eyes closed. After the wound from the bullet graze had been tended and a complete exam finished, he hadn't left her side.

Refused to leave until he saw those beautiful brown eyes open.

She hadn't woken since she'd slipped into unconsciousness on her way to the ambulance. There was no medical reason why she shouldn't be awake. All that was left to do was wait and pray and pour every ounce of positive energy into her that he could.

"How's she doing?"

The raw emotion in Mike's voice matched what Cody felt. He glanced up at the older man and swore he'd aged in the last hour that they'd been there.

Cody cleared his throat and kept a firm grip on Katherine's hand. "Vitals look good. She's all stitched up. Now all we need is for her to open her eyes."

Mike kept his gaze locked on Katherine's face. "She will. Just give her a little time."

"Any word on Keith Stiller? Did he talk when Owen got him to the station?" He couldn't bring himself to really care about anyone else right now, but he asked anyway.

"Told Owen everything, and you were spot on. He blamed her for his arrest. Thought she'd told me, and I'd sent in the cops. Her face was the only one that stood out to him, and he spent fifteen years being angry at the wrong person."

"And Katherine paid the cost." He was too tired, too scared, to be angry. That would come later.

A hand on his shoulder lifted his gaze. "I'm going to see Ollie. He's chomping at the bit to see his mom, but I think it'd be better if she's awake when he visits. I'll tell him as much as I can. Let me know as soon as she opens her eyes."

"I will."

Mike leaned down to kiss Katherine's cheek. "Come back to us, sweetheart. We love you."

Cody waited for her father to leave before focusing all his attention back on Katherine. "Did you hear that? Your dad's going to see Ollie. It's going to take a small army to keep that kid away from you. He was pretty scared. It'd be better if you were awake when he got here."

Her finger moved a fraction in his hand, and he sat up straighter. She'd wake up eventually for everyone, but she'd fight the hardest for her son.

"He's with Elsie now. Bailey went with him. That's the only way I could get him to leave my house. I'm not sure I'll get Bailey to come home without him. You might have to adopt an over-eager Bernedoodle when you get out of here."

Her eyes fluttered open, and the hint of a smile lifted the side of her mouth. "No way."

Relief expanded his chest. He pressed the hand he still held to his lips then tucked a slip of hair behind her ears. Standing, he leaned over her, resisting the urge to climb into the bed and gather her in his arms. "I won't tell her you said that. It might hurt her feelings."

Her grin grew. "We need a reason to visit you." Her voice was dry and low, and she lifted her fingers to the base of her bruised neck. "Hurts."

"Don't talk. Save your strength. My God, Katherine, I've never been so damn scared in my entire life. When I ran into that house and found him on you, I nearly died myself. But you're a fighter. That was clear in the blood and bruises you left on Keith."

"Is he gone?"

"Gone forever. You and Ollie can go home and forget this ever happened. Life can go back to normal." The words were like chalk in his mouth, but he needed her to know that no matter what she decided to do from here on out, all that mattered was that she was safe.

That she was happy.

Her smile fell and tears hovered on her lashes and slid over her cheeks.

"Hey, now," he said, brushing away the tears with the pad of his thumb. "It's all over. You don't need to be afraid anymore."

Lifting a shaky hand, she covered his knuckles with her palm and anchored it against her cheek. "Not scared. So sorry," she whispered, wincing.

"We don't need to talk about that right now."

She shook her head, then squeezed her eyes shut for a beat before setting them on him once again. "You matter. To me and Ollie. I love you, Cody."

She opened her mouth to say more but he stopped her with a kiss. Talking was the last thing she needed to be doing, and there was nothing more he needed to hear.

"I love you, too, Katherine. I was afraid I'd never get a

chance to tell you. It's fast as hell, and I don't know how I got so lucky, but I love you and that kid of yours so damn much."

A soft tap at the door drew his attention to Jenna.

"Glad to see you're awake," Jenna said. "How are you feeling?"

"Sore, but not too bad," Katherine said, a smile fixed on her beautiful face.

"I want you to stay overnight for observation. Especially since you lost consciousness." Jenna studied a tablet before glancing at the machines next to the bed. "Everything else looks good. Just take it easy for a few days. Your stitches are the least of your worries. The head wound will leave you nauseous, possibly dizzy, and the headache will linger for a while. Stick with liquids and soft foods until your throat feels better. Wouldn't hurt to have someone help you until you're one hundred percent."

"I'm on it," Cody said. "Between you and Ollie, I'll get some nursing skills of my own."

Jenna grinned. "Looking forward to hearing about that. Let me know if you need anything while you're here."

Cody waited for Jenna to leave before reclaiming his seat besides Katherine. "You okay with me taking care of you for a while?"

"I wouldn't want it any other way."

"Good, because I plan on doing it for a very long time."

She lifted her arms. "Hold me?"

"Always." He moved with care as he circled his arms around her and held her close. He kissed the side of her face, up to her forehead then briefly touched her lips with his.

And everything shifted into place, his heart and arms full and his future filled with wonderful possibilities.

THREE MONTHS LATER, the summer heat beat down on Katherine as she carried her last box out of the moving truck. Her muscles burned and exhaustion slowed her steps up the walkway toward Cody's house. It'd been a long, emotional day. One that was as difficult as it was exciting.

Cody jogged outside. "Here, let me get that." He took the box from her and led the way back inside.

Stacked boxes greeted her in the living room.

Ollie ran down the hall and gave her a huge hug, Bailey right behind him.

"I'm not sure who's more excited about move-in day," she said with a small laugh. "You or Bailey."

"Me, for sure!" Ollie gave her one more squeeze then threw his arms around the dog's furry neck. "I finally have a dog."

Cody's warm chuckle covered her like a soft blanket. "I hope it's not just the dog you're excited about."

"Are you kidding?" Ollie asked. "My new room is so cool." In a flash, he was back down the hall, disappearing into his room with his dog at his side.

Katherine leaned against Cody and sighed. "You sure you can handle us?"

"I have no doubt." He kissed the top of her head. "You sure you're okay with selling your house? I know it means a lot to you. You have a lot of memories wrapped up in that place."

She turned to face him, circling her arms around his waist and resting her head on his chest. "Memories stay with us no matter where we are. Ollie and I needed a fresh start, and your place feels like home."

He held her tight. "You feel like home."

She grinned up at him. "Right back at ya."

"I just hope this space is big enough. I didn't realize how much stuff you two had."

She laughed. "We'll find a place for it. It just might take a while."

"We have all the time in the world." He stepped back and whistled. "Ollie, you ready?"

"If you think he's going to help put all this stuff away, you're in for a big surprise. I'll be impressed if he can figure out how to put his own clothes in the closet."

Ollie and Bailey bounded back down the hall. Ollie's ear-to-ear grin had her on high alert.

"What's going on?"

Ollie stopped in front of her and took hold of one of her hands then grabbed one of Cody's. "Ready."

Cody captured Katherine's free hand, creating a little circle amidst the chaos around them. "Ollie and I had a very important talk last night."

Ollie nodded his head up and down in an exaggerated motion. "We sure did."

"I wanted to make sure he was comfortable moving in here. That he knew this was his home in every way and that his being here made me happier than I ever thought possible."

Katherine's heart stuttered. She hadn't taken this step lightly, and there'd been many conversations with her, Ollie, and Cody about what was best for all of them. But the fact that Cody had spoken with Ollie on his own solidified that she'd made the right decision.

"I told him I was happy," Ollie said, as if it wasn't obvious.

"We also talked about being a family," Cody continued.

The air left Katherine's lungs and she squeezed Cody's hand.

"I made it clear that I'll never take the place of his father, but that I'd like to be there for him if he needs anything. Ever. That I can be whoever he wants, as long he knows I love him and want the best for him."

Ollie's chest puffed out.

"And," Cody continued. "I asked him if he would be okay if we made this little family official."

"I said yes." Ollie rolled his eyes. "Why wouldn't I want that?"

A sob caught in Katherine's throat. She didn't know if she wanted to cry at the sweetness of Cody's words or laugh at her child's reaction to it all.

"You're supposed to wait to tell her that," Cody stage whispered then let go of her hand to reach into his pocket. He pulled out a black velvet box and dropped to one knee. "I have Ollie's permission to ask you this. Katherine Milton, you've been one hell of a surprise that I'll forever be grateful for. You brought love and hope and happiness into my life."

"And me!" Ollie chimed in.

Cody laugh. "Yes, and Ollie. Would you make me the happiest man on the planet and be my wife?"

Tears fell down her cheeks. She brought Ollie's hand to her lips and kissed it before letting go and dropping to her knees in front of Cody. "I'd be honored to be your wife. Thank you for loving me and my son. I love you so much."

He slipped the princess cut diamond onto her finger and grinned. "Good job, Ollie." He lifted his fist and waited for the little boy to tap it with his own before standing and sweeping her off her feet.

Laughing, she held on tight until he set her down. She looped one arm around Ollie and stared at the ring then back at the man who'd be her husband. The man who'd opened his heart to her and her child and shown her that life might hand out surprises, but if you let it, those surprises can turn into the biggest blessings of all.

EPILOGUE

Staring into the full-length mirror, Katherine smoothed the front of her knee-length ivory dress. The V neck and cinched waist showed off her curves while the full skirt kept everything demure and elegant. She wore her long hair down and jewelry minimal—diamond studs in her ears and her engagement ring on her left hand.

The fabric flower attached to the satin bow tied around her waist was made from her first wedding dress. A simple way to keep Theo a part of her new family.

Marie and Sadie stood on each side of her with tears in their eyes.

A lot of things were different about her second wedding, but having her new sisters with her was one of the best parts.

"You look beautiful," Marie said, giving her a quick hug.

"Stunning," Sadie agreed. She handed over the bouquet of calla lilies wrapped in a blush pink ribbon. "You guys pulled this wedding off in record time."

"Ollie wouldn't have it any other way." She brought the flowers to her nose and drew in a deep breath. The sweet fragrance overwhelmed her senses. "Doesn't hurt that we decided to get married in the backyard. It's the only place where Bailey was allowed to attend."

As if saying her son's name summoned him, Ollie bounded inside with Bailey at his heels.

Her heart melted at the sight of his white button up shirt and black suspenders. He'd tied a matching bow around Bailey's neck.

"You look pretty, Mom." He ran and gave her a big hug. "Grandpa says it's time."

Grinning, she rolled her eyes. It was her day, but she was still on her dad's schedule. "Well, where is he? I need you both to walk me down the aisle."

Sadie laid a hand on her arm and squeezed. "I'll send him in. Marie and I will find our seats. See you out there."

Grateful for the moment alone with her son, she held out her hand for him to take. "You look very handsome. Your daddy would have loved to see you all dressed up."

He twisted his lips to the side. "But if Daddy was here, I wouldn't be dressed up because you wouldn't be marrying Cody."

"That's true."

"I miss Daddy, but I love Cody," he said, frowning. "It's kinda confusing."

"It's confusing at times for me too, but that doesn't mean we can't be happy about this next step. Daddy would want that. For both of us." She believed that with her entire heart. Theo would always be there, his memory forever shaping her and Ollie's lives. But Cody was the leading man in her next chapter. She didn't have to understand it, she just had to be grateful for the second chance at love.

"I am happy," he said.

Bailey barked in agreement.

"Me, too buddy. And I love you so much. Thank you for always being the favorite part of my day."

Ollie's expression crumbled in concern. "You better not tell Cody that. At least not today. He should be your favorite part."

She laughed and ruffled his hair before placing a kiss on the top of his head. "Fair point."

The sound of a clearing throat drew her attention to the doorway. Her dad stood there dressed in a black suit and matching tie. He held out his arm. "Ready?"

"Ready." She took hold of Ollie's hand then looped her arm through her dad's.

The trio walked out the backdoor and the wedding march played from speakers hidden somewhere down below. They descended the stairs and her gaze drifted down the aisle the second her foot hit the grass.

White chairs filled the lawn with a runner dividing them down the middle. Friends and family stood and watched her every step as she moved along with her dad and son. Owen and Tommy sat with Marie and Sadie in the front row—Amelia and Nora wearing matching pink dresses. Pappy leaned on his cane beside Marie with tears in his eyes.

Mrs. Collins hooked an arm through Laura's, Cade and Isla at Laura's other side. Jenna and Calvin watched alongside Elsie and Dean. Jimmy and Oliver waving at Ollie with grins on their little faces. Clara and Heath held hands while Avery and Davey whispered beside them.

But it was the man at the end of the aisle that captured her attention.

Cody stood tall and more handsome than she'd ever seen with his white button up shirt. He'd rolled his sleeves to his elbows and opted for no tie, leaving the collar open. His eyes stayed focused on her as she made her way past everyone she loved to get to his side.

Her dad pressed a kiss to her cheek. "I love you, honey. Be happy."

"Thanks, Dad."

Ollie stayed beside her, both of them facing Cody.

Cody grabbed her free hand and grazed his thumb over her skin, sending ripples of goosebumps cascading over her body despite the summer sun. "You look beautiful."

She grinned. "You're not too shabby yourself."

"What about me?" Ollie asked, gaining a chuckle from the crowd.

"Looking good, Dude." Cody held up his free palm for a high five.

Ollie slapped his hand. "Can I sit with Bailey now?"

Katherine chuckled. "Sure." She waited for her son to sit on a chair by Pappy with Bailey on the other side before facing Cody.

The minister began the ceremony, the words of love and commitment floating by as she kept her eyes locked on Cody. Her body vibrated with excitement when he slipped the wedding ring on her finger, and she did the same for him.

"You may now kiss the bride," the minister shouted, invoking a chorus of cheers.

Cody wrapped her in his arms and grinned down at her. "I love you, Mrs. Hogan. Now and forever. You'll always have my heart. Thank you for giving me a family."

Happiness exploded inside her and tears glistened in her eyes, blurring her vision. "I love you, too, Mr. Hogan. And I'm so glad you're happy about our family because it's about to get a little bigger."

His jaw dropped. "Seriously?"

Tears streamed down her face, and she nodded.

He let out a whoop of joy then crushed his mouth to hers.

She melted against him, memorizing every touch, every taste, every feel of this wonderful man who'd fallen into her life when she'd least expected it. She'd never understand how she'd gotten so lucky—found real, strong love twice in a lifetime.

And now she had that whole lifetime ahead of her to make countless memories with her handsome husband, amazing child, and a baby on the way.

Life was good, and she'd make sure to never, ever forget it.

~

DON'T MISS out on an exciting new series! In Hard to Break, a bull-riding wreck sends Lane Tipton back to the town he swore off, he's forced to face the woman—and the secret—he left behind. But when danger closes in, their second chance might be their last.

ACKNOWLEDGMENTS

As much as I loved writing Katherine and Cody's story, it was so hard knowing this was the end of the road for the Safe Haven Women's Shelter series. This series has been such a labor of love, and has changed not only my career, but my life.

Being able to complete this series with the last Wells sibling was a special treat. Getting another look at Pappy made me so happy. I loved seeing all the familiar faces and knowing I'm leaving this world with everyone filled with happiness and hope.

As always, thank you to my husband and children for their support. To my amazing critique partner, Samantha Wilde, as well The Editing Soprano and Deranged Doctors for their editing and covers. And thank you most to my readers! Thank you for reading this series!

Danielle

ABOUT THE AUTHOR

Danielle M Haas is a stay-at-home mom turned author. When she isn't writing fast-paced romantic suspense novels with mysteries to live for and romance to die for, she's busy being a taxi driver to her two busy kids and forcing her introverted self to talk to other soccer moms. Her kids and husband are her world, which is also shared with her hyper Bernie doodle, mini Whoodle, and two sassy cats. Her days are packed with cuddles, kisses, and a brain constantly thinking of new ways to create danger and romance for her next book.

Sign up for Danielle's NEWSLETTER to stay up to date with everything she has going on.

ALSO BY DANIELLE HAAS

The Sheffield's Series

Second Time Around

A Place In This World

Coming Home

Stand Alones

Bound by Danger

Girl Long Gone

www.ingramcontent.com/pod-product-compliance
Lightning Source LLC
Chambersburg PA
CBHW022149240626
47153CB00007B/2573